More praise for *Nature and Other Mothers*

"Whether about a dolphin, tree, landscape, or a family member, Peterson writes with an awe-inspired aptitude for learning from it rather than teaching it a lesson. To claim kinship rather than difference or dominion is an earnest challenge for Peterson; it must be for us readers, too. But we have the advantage of this author's nurturing—I'd judiciously say *mothering* if we could all be big boys and girls who would relish, rather than resent, such tendered concern."

> —Michael J. Rosen
> Editor of *The Company of Cats*
> and *The Company of Dogs*

"A lyrical and life-enhancing collection . . . There are large doses of wonder, humor and warmth . . . *Nature and Other Mothers* is overflowing with heartening and healing spiritual thoughts."
> —*Values & Visions*

"Moving but never sentimental, sophisticated but accessible, this small volume is sure to both inspire and amuse. Highly recommended."

> —*Library Journal*

"Mesmerizing . . . Beautifully written."

> —*Moving Words*

NATURE AND
OTHER MOTHERS

PERSONAL STORIES OF WOMEN
AND THE BODY OF
EARTH

BRENDA PETERSON

To Paulette
a natural woman
with the hope that someday
we'll ~~meet~~ meet.

Yours,

Brenda Peterson

FAWCETT COLUMBINE
New York

A Fawcett Columbine Book
Published by Ballantine Books

Acknowledgments of sources follow page 177.

Library of Congress Catalog Card Number: 95-90152

ISBN: 0-449-90967-0

Cover design by Kristine Mills
Cover photo by Lisa Whitsitt, tinted by Sandee Cohen
Text design by Debby Jay

Manufactured in the United States of America
First Ballantine Books Trade Paperback Edition: September 1995
10 9 8 7 6 5 4 3 2 1

for

BETH, SUSAN, PAULA, AND KATHERINE,
who each in her own way
has mothered this book

CONTENTS

ACKNOWLEDGMENTS

I would like to gratefully acknowledge my friend Joe Meeker, for lending me the title from his original essay "Nature and Other Mothers," first written as a Mother's Day present for his wife, Maureen, and published in the journal *Between the Species* (Winter 1984). Deep thanks also to Flor Fernandez for her insightful support; to Susan Biskeborn, my fabulous first reader; to Louise Bode for listening; to Rebecca Lisa Romanelli for inspired play; to Linda Boudreau for wise nurturing; to my students for their heartfelt dialogue; to Rebecca Wells for an astute final editorial read; to Christine Lamb for her artistic expertise; and to Peggy Taylor for her loyal guidance in assigning many of these nature essays. In this paperback edition, I'd also like to thank Joanne Wyckoff for her deep and heartfelt editing, Andrea Schulz for her kind efficiency, and my own assistant, Becca Robinson, for her wonderful weekly midwifery of my work.

The Tao is called the Great Mother:
* empty yet inexhaustible,*
* it gives birth to infinite worlds.*
It is always present within you.
You can use it any way you want.

—Lao-Tzu, Tao Te Ching
* (Stephen Mitchell translation)*

Nature and Other Mothers

Introduction

Nature was my first mother — the fragrant, old forests of the Sierra Nevada mountains near the California-Oregon border, where my father worked on the Plumas National Forest. Living in a rough-hewn Forest Service cabin on vast acres of fir, mysterious blue spruce, and ponderosa pine, I memorized the forest floor as I would my mother's body. This forest skin smelled like pine sap and sweet rot, and it stained my diapers green and perfumed my hair, which was always tangled with bits of leaves, small sticks, and moss. It never occurred to me during those early years in the forest that I was human.

When I crawled through whispering cedars and redwoods which my father—himself part-Seminole and part-Swede—called the Standing People, those attentive trees recognized me as perhaps another bobcat or burrowing bear cub, my small paws imprinted with pine needles and pungent dirt. Before I learned words, I listened to the piercing language of hawks and hoot owls, of thunder cracking tree limbs. In the clearing outside our circled cabins, we were surrounded by the curves of boulders. On their warm, stone breasts I could sun myself, bare bellied or curled like a snake. In the forest, skin was anything that embraced me—soft, decaying Earth or muddy riverbank, slick ferns or even the sweet, rambling touch of honeysuckle. Sometimes this dense mother of Earth had skin that glowed green or musty brown; often her hair was high, pale grasses. When I lay upon her I felt again a great heartbeat throbbing. I knew then before any human ever whispered the words to me, that I was loved by nature, as I first loved her.

Our small tribe of foresters and their families also did not seem separate or, to my child's eye, distinct from the forest. Until my sister arrived when I was two, there were no other children, so animals were my first brothers and sisters. I chattered away with squirrels and nodded with woodpeckers; I engaged in long dialogues with guardian garden snakes and even a rattler. I sensed the light-hooved elk and deer whose eyes sometimes shone out from the trees like burning spirits. I listened to knotholes and beavers, to pine cones and river rapids. For years I was barely aware of the fast, high chatter of the few humans around me.

The forest was my father's office; our log cabin belonged to my mother. Because my mother was a town girl whom my father had wooed away from her wild, Wabash railroading ways; because my mother was a would-be writer who, in her own words, "had babies instead of books," I grew up with two especially strong sounds in my mind: my mother's typewriter tapping out words and waves of high-mountain wind through tall trees.

Even after my mother's typewriter fell silent and many of the trees in my father's forest had begun to fall, the wilderness remained within me. I am imprinted by nature more deeply than any mark will ever make on this Earth. Because of that original body-bond, I have never been able to separate myself from nature. And because I am female, I still recognize that the umbilical link, once nurtured, is never really broken. It is a lifelong, physical connection.

Even when my family first left the forest to follow my father's forestry career all over this country, I did not leave nature behind. Though he worked in cities, my father always planted his family in surrounding countrysides—across the street from the Atlantic Ocean in Massachusetts, on the Yellow River in Georgia, nestled in Montana meadows, perched high on California canyons, and then in the gentle forests of Virginia. One of my most enduring childhood memories is of running full tilt through the piney Virginia woods, screaming or neighing, depending upon whether my siblings and I were humans or horses. Sometimes we refused to speak any human language, preferring instead animal calls and codes.

Nature was never a place we visited as if we didn't belong. It was not a park or well-kept yard. It was our habitat, wild, tender and terrible—like the time a tornado lifted me off my feet or when lightning snatched a tree right next to me and tore it into black, twisted pieces. Nor was nature simply a backdrop to our human dramas; nature herself was most often the main event and we the awestruck spectators. My father was one of the first on the scene of the Montana Earthquake in Gallatin National Forest in 1959; he took us to see the aftermath—roads split into asphalt shards, houses floating upside down in the swift floodwaters, gigantic trees snapped like tinder, and cracks in the Earth like chasms. "Well," my father explained with a shake of his head, "when the Earth starts shaking, people got to move, too."

We moved all over this country as children, following my father's forestry work, but what always stayed with us was that sense of the power and grace of the natural world. None of my younger siblings has ever lived in any place longer than five years, in keeping with our transient childhoods. But in 1982, when I first saw Puget Sound in Seattle, I felt again the physical recognition that I first felt in the forest—here was a natural teacher to instruct and enchant. So here I have stayed, near this inland sea's wide and welcoming embrace.

...with Puget Sound, my chosen natural
...prenticeship to the water, the animals,
... It is from them that I learn how to be
... book explores many natural teachers who
... minds and bodies—both human and nonhu-
... book's first publication in 1992, I have made
more ... ging explorations into that territory of the feminine and nature. And everywhere I have looked—from our
sensual lives to our relationships with animals to our storytelling—I have found that the life-giving link between women
and the body of Earth is being reclaimed.

In fact, new research has revealed the astonishing yet somehow familiar fact that within women an innate circadian clock
changes with the seasons. Unlike men, women experience a
seasonal hormonal shift that can be measured by changes in
the secretion of melatonin. So even our female bodies are in
sync with the body of Earth as we reflect physically the ebb
and flow of changing sunlight and seasons. This physical connection grounds women's bodies in the Earth's ancient cycles.
We only have to listen to our bodies to reestablish this intimacy with nature.

As a woman whose birthplace was wilderness, I often look
to animals as my teachers, in the way that I believe nature was
my first mother. Sometimes I am surprised at the discrepancy
between the animal or natural world and my human species.
For example, when I study animals in nature, such as the dolphins I've been swimming with for the last decade, I've been
impressed with the sheer strength and power of animal mothers. A dolphin mother or aunt swimming within the pod's
nursery will attack any shark who approaches a dolphin calf.
At speeds of up to 40 m.p.h., the female dolphin will repeatedly ram the shark's soft underbelly with her strong beak, until
the shark bleeds to death from internal hemorrhaging. In the
animal kingdom this is seen as a natural, protective, inbred

survival skill to assure a next generation. In human species, there is such fear of strong women that women who are powerful must continually deny, pacify, and play down their strengths instead of claiming them as a birthright.

In ancient times, primitive societies recognized divinities as female and often animal. Some hunter-gatherer groups, for instance, worshipped the mother bear as a deity. Over the centuries, though, the link between women and nature has eroded. Women have borne much in the way of domination and disfigurement, of domestication and attempts to cut us off from our natures. Like any occupied territory, whether forest or female body, the feminine to be restored must begin by recovering our origins and roots. Then we can imagine what we will become, when that umbilical cord between our bodies and the Earth is again strongly nurturing us.

This book is meant to nurture through story. I have organized the book into two sections. In the first part, "Women and the Body of Earth," I've gathered together a decade of stories centered on what it means to be in communion with the feminine—what skills, insights, and gifts women offer to ourselves and the world. In the second section, "Nature and Other Mothers," I've expanded that feminine relationship to include nature and other nonhuman animals. The new stories in this book include "Sex as Compassion—A New Eros in a Time of AIDS," "Animal Allies," "Beluga Baby," and "Seagull Song." All of these stories were written out of the strong feeling that storytelling is not only a healing link between ourselves and other species, but also a way of connecting based on compassionate respect for what might otherwise be seen as Other. Nothing outside us, even a terrible disease, is alien if it is recognized as somehow connected to us. And discovering those sometimes difficult, other times inspiring connections is what these new stories seek.

Because my first mother was nature, I know I can return to

...urance and strength, as well as for inspiration and ...ns on how to be human—that is, of the Earth, the ...r matter. I also know that deeper than the concept of ...vation or stewardship or environmentalism, which is rooted in humans heroically going outward and "saving" the Earth, is the simple love of the natural world. Loving nature in return for her abundance and support is what every child does when he or she stretches out her arms to the ocean, climbs a favorite tree, explores a cave. Love of nature implies intimacy and relationship. Instead of saving, we might consider surrendering to this wondrous Earth which is our only home. In giving ourselves over to a nature that is so much greater than ourselves, we remember our early ancestors' devotion and spiritual embrace of this Earth and all her creatures.

Direct experience of the natural world reminds us that we are literally made of Earth—that she is our skin, our body. Many of the stories in this book are in praise of that luminous skin we share. Other stories are simply in praise of nature, even in the face of so much extinction and pollution.

There are times as a nature writer and storyteller when I feel the despair of our environmental destruction; but this grief, too, is holy and healing to the Earth. One spring evening in 1989, after hearing of the terrible Exxon-Valdez oil spill in Alaska's Prince William Sound, I felt so heartsick, so ashamed of my own species and our perpetual degradation of this beautiful world, that I took myself down to my backyard beach on Puget Sound. As I sat on a driftwood log staring out into the Sound at dusk, I felt a distinct pull onto the wet sand—like a kind of gravity reaching up for me from the Earth. Without thinking, I lay down on the warm, yielding sand and soon found my body naturally curling into fetal curves. It was very old, this memory of a heartbeat pulsing through the Earth into my own body, but it was as if I had never left, once I returned, ear to the ground. Against this grainy skin, my cheeks were im-

printed with small pebbles and shells. Eye-level with the barna-
cled mussels and seaweed, I watched anemones squirt tiny geysers as if in rhythm to underground music. Waves lapped
closer and closer to my face and their shushing was deeper
than any lullaby. I listened and that familiar embrace reminded
me—my body of this Earth was loved as I loved. I was home,
held deeply by my first and last mother. And this was human
nature.

PART I

WOMEN AND THE BODY OF EARTH

In Praise of Skin

For R.L.R.

In the snowy Seattle winter of 1985, after a month of high fevers and strep throat, I sat amid the holiday hubbub of our Thanksgiving table and noticed my hands and arms were breaking out in spots. By the time we were drinking our hot toddies before the fire, there were spots between my toes, lightly marching across my face, up and down my legs.

In the course of the next week I was given three diagnoses. The emergency room declared my spots an allergy to antibiotics, my doctor suggested *psi roseola* or *guttate psoriasis*, and Southern friends recognized it surely as "fever rash," a children's disease. For the next few months I went around looking like a thirty-five-year-old woman with chicken pox. Incurable, they said; it'll come and go. My doctor called in an "unlimited" prescription for cortisone cream. At night my housemate played dot-to-dot, dabbing the expensive cream on my back. Slowly the spots faded, only to return when I drank coffee or played racquetball. Stress-related, someone suggested. Maybe I was allergic to my own adrenaline?

I called my sister, a surgical nurse and mother of three girls. "I'm trying to imagine how you look with all those spots," she said. "Is it like when you sat on that wasps' nest at Grandad and Vergie's and got stung all over? Remember Vergie's cure?"

Of course I remembered—screaming in the front yard with welts swelling everywhere while my grandfather spat tobacco juice as a poultice until Vergie swooped me up in her arms and carried me to the metal tub in her farmhouse kitchen. Even in Vergie's arms, deep in the cool comfrey bath, my body felt flensed, too raw to touch. Yet Vergie kept running her hands all over, lightly cooing, shushing, talking to my skin as if tenderly telling it that now was a safe time to come back.

Then this stepgrandmother, who for many years had followed her beauty shop clients from her Cut 'n' Curl pink swivel chairs to the steel tables of the local morgue, where she moonlighted as a beautician, confided in me a secret ritual. "Your body's skin," Vergie said, "is harder-working and more wide open than the human heart; it's a sad thing to see how skin gets passed right over, barely touched except in sex, or sickness, or deep trouble. Why, we pay so little mind to our own skin, we might as well be living inside a foreign country."

Then she told me another secret. She considered it an honor and a sacred death chore to touch every inch of skin on a body before it was buried, just the way she was touching me now in my healing bath.

This ritual had come to Vergie when Edna Crow died. Edna had just called to schedule a set and blue rinse, but Vergie met her in the morgue for their appointment. She'd long ago memorized Edna's head from many scalp massages during shampoos. And between the foot washings and laying-on-of-hands in church, the midwifing strokes and massages during Edna's three long labors, there was hardly a bit of Edna's body that Vergie didn't already know.

She also knew that Edna, widowed for decades, hadn't been touched in the simple, selfless petting that, as Vergie points out, "babies and even barnyard cats get." So it was Mrs. Crow in the stillness of the mortuary who received Vergie's first beautification ritual. Lightly, with dignity and recognition, Vergie ran her hands along those old limbs, touched each worn fingertip, held that big toe that was once broken by a runaway grocery cart, and finally cupped that familiar head in her palms like a favorite bowl.

That day in Vergie's tub as she told me her secrets and stories, my skin healed so deeply that all the wasp sting spots were gone by morning.

"Yes," I told my sister, staring at my own hands again covered with spots. "I remember Vergie's cures."

"Well," my sister suggested softly, "Vergie would say you need some simple mothering." She laughed. "You need a good rubdown, baby." Thus I began a regimen of cool comfrey baths alternating with hot eucalyptus rubs.

All my life I'd followed Vergie's hands-on tradition by massaging the heads and feet of my family and friends. Now I set up a series of trades with two massage therapist friends: I worked on their heads and they on my skin. We tried everything that winter, but my mysterious spots would vanish and then reappear with their own logic. Then someone suggested that along with the baths and massage, I alternate racquetball with a more meditative exercise; why not try yoga, long known as a way of cleansing the body?

So one icy January evening my friend Gregory Bolton, a massage instructor at Seattle Massage School, and I attended our first yoga class. As I practiced the postures I felt my aching, raw skin expand, stretch, then release with my muscles—almost as if the skin itself were breathing.

My first yoga teacher, Rebecca Romanelli, a deep-tissue therapist, told me about the fourth chakra of the heart, traditionally associated with the sense of touch. "Skin is the body's biggest organ," she reminded me. "It breathes, filters, and protects. It's more important than the heart. Someone with a third of his heart blocked can still live and breathe—but if a body loses a third of its skin, it dies."

That spring, as the spots faded from my face, I began to study the *skin of things*: cool green watermelon rinds, the graceful flap of cornstalks and silks; green, cupped palms of cabbage heads, red chrysalides of ripe tomatoes; the scarlet peel of pomegranate, symbol of immortality or—for Persephone—a season in the underworld. I found myself studying animal skin, running my hands along the tanned, soft hides that were our species' first mythical and physical survival—to hide inside the body of a greater animal, for warmth, for camouflage, to borrow spiritual power.

One summer night during another bout with fever and spots, I had a dream. All around me stood ancient Chinese doctors, men and women, their faces fragile as rice paper, skin luminous as the translucent surface of water when the sun shines on it just so. They were laughing and running their hands up and down my body. I recognized Vergie among them; then I relaxed, resting as they smiled and raised their robed arms. On their sleeves were brilliant symbols and moving pictographs. All the while they ran those beautiful, tapered hands up and down my body, I lay beneath them, laughing. When I awoke my fever had broken and my spots were almost completely gone.

Perhaps it was the laughter—something I'd been in short supply of that year-of-the-spots. I remember that morning after my dream as one might a hallucination. All my senses heightened, I ran my hands along my clear belly, my arms and legs, my at last unblemished brow. I felt a radiant well-being, as if I'd grown new skin in the night. It was the way a snake must feel when it finally slithers free from what it once believed it could not live without, only to find a glowing, new expanse of skin.

· · ·

Over the next years I continued yoga and massage work; learning to be at home in my own body, and sensually more at home with other bodies, be they male or female companions. But not until recently did I come to realize that the Chinese-doctor dream had to do with larger healing. Another friend, Bettelinn Krizek Brown, who has practiced massage and yoga for over eighteen years, introduced me to a ritual that reunited me with Vergie's hands-on tradition.

Called *jin shin jytsu* or "the art of compassionate being," this ancient Oriental healing art was originally practiced not by doctors but in the home. Long ago in China the *jin shin* laying on of hands was anchored to oral formulas, stories that have since been lost. But the physical practice was rediscovered by Master Jiro Murai of Japan, who in turn taught it to Mary Ino Burmeister, who brought it to this country. My own teacher, Betsy Dayton, founder of the High Touch Network in Friday Harbor, Washington, studied with Burmeister and has had her own practice for fourteen years.

Jin shin is a *yin* or feminine approach to the hands-on healing tradition. Like acupuncture, the art follows the ancient Oriental meridians of energy in the body; but since *jin shin* uses only the deep, electromagnetic energy of the human hands, it is not intrusive like the *yang* or masculine, projectile approach of needles. It is also feminine in that there is no exchange of energy, but more a support for the body to tap into its own energy and unblock the various pressure points. Fluid and subtle, yet powerful, the acupressure treatments are called "flows" and the *jin shin* hands learn to see and listen to the body's pulses.

In *jin shin*, the skin symbolizes a level of energy cycling associated with the lung and large intestine, the element of metal, the color white, the sound of weeping, the season of autumn, the very early morning, and the emotion of grief. According to these ancients, grief is the first emotion one must learn, the moment one recognizes his or her own separate skin. But this experience can lead to a physical epiphany. Skin need not be some earthly prison—it is the way a soul may choose to experience, to feel, and finally to embody what on a spiritual level one might already know. And perhaps this is what it is to be human: to reach out for warmth, for light, for another skin with the part of oneself that is the most tangible, the most vulnerable, the most mortal.

Finally, every inch of skin's embrace is a self-regulating, self-healing system. Recent medical research supports this more intuitive understanding in its discovery that skin plays a previously unsuspected and crucial role in maintaining the body's biochemistry, and that the skin's role in producing interferons is vital to a healthy immune system.

It is sad and curious that our biggest health fear, an epidemic of AIDS, has to do not with a plaguelike virus or inner misfiring of cells like cancer but a breaking of skin. We have upon us a disease that redefines lovemaking from strictly intercourse to two bodies simply being together. We are in a sexual age that throws us back on touch. Touching one another in that abiding ritual distinct from sex is something other centuries knew all about. But we moderns have much to learn or, as the Chinese doctors reminded me, to remember.

Our sexual revolution's anchor of skin and touch strictly to sex is a deep impoverishment. Amid our society's expanse of exposed skin, the flaunt of flesh, we are not really touched, known, memorized in what was Vergie's tradition. In fact, many of my massage therapist friends tell me they know more about their clients' bodies than their husbands or wives or lovers. "A shame," Vergie would say, "a crying shame." And it's the hands that are crying.

When I'm working with my hands these days, I think of Vergie. She is the only person I know who if blinded could recognize an old lover, her husband, her children, her stepfamily, and all her clients by hand.

Perhaps it will take us all our lives to fully possess our own and recognize others' skin. In doing so, we might well practice in Vergie's hands-on tradition: a deep attention to skin that is a healing art, that abides with the body and has no expectations, no goals—not lovemaking, not changing, not correcting this or that muscle or bone, but just *being with* another's body, memorizing its pulses and curves and hollows as if hands could hear and see and somehow let be, even while embracing.

Sex as Compassion— A New Eros in a Time of AIDS

When I was nineteen and in my freshman year at the University of California, Davis, I took part in a 1968 experimental program called "Self and Society." Inspired by the '60s novel *The Harrad Experiment*, our program included sexual relations studies and introduced the college's first co-ed dorm, with males and females sharing everything from bathrooms to bedrooms. Oddly enough, familiarity between the sexes bred neither contempt nor couples; instead, most of us found ourselves living side by side like siblings. Out of the two hundred young men and women in my dorm, there were only five or six couples; the rest found romance outside our sociology program.

My boyfriend, Daniel, and I were one of those few couples who met sharing the same bathroom mirror, he shaving and I putting on makeup. Daniel was from Hawaii, part-Polynesian, with lustrous black curls I imagined twirling around my fingers long before I ever touched him. He was dark-skinned, his face wide open and his body muscular, compact. Dreamy and imaginative, he could play more deeply than anyone I had ever met. In a dorm where every exit stairwell was filled with drug deals, antiwar folksingers, or intense encounters of the psychological kind, Daniel and I would escape to his room and read novels together. We'd act out the dialogue and love scenes. Sometimes we'd even switch gender roles, taking turns playing virile hero and shy virgin. We were, in fact, both virgins. I was on the health clinic's waiting list for birth control pills and was very afraid of pregnancy in this time of illegal abortions. Daniel did not trust condoms, having himself been born as a result of that more risky method. We both wanted the protection of the pill. This meant that for four months we would have to figure out how to make love without intercourse.

One day Daniel showed me an old Chinese Taoist pillow book he had found in Hawaii. It was an instructional manual usually given to newlyweds for practicing sexual arts. Illustrated with elegant watercolors and indecipherable Chinese characters, the book did have one English inscription in delicate penmanship: "Practice with careful tenderness. Breathe together."

We lay propped up over the exquisite picture book: Here were couples gazing tenderly into each other's dark eyes, their delicate limbs entwined in elegant postures of worship, abandon, and surrender as they stroked thighs, toes, bellies, gently sloped backs, or graceful buttocks. Their sensual play was artful, their bedrooms adorned with silken beds and painted scrolls—a brilliant, mineral blue-green seascape, a benevolent Taoist master's portrait serenely watching over the lovers. Our favorite picture was a couple in a garden, languid willow falling over their pallet as the woman lay back, contented and trusting, against the man's chest. Embracing her from behind, his hands held her breasts as if they were the most precious porcelain vases held up to golden daylight. At her feet a pink lotus burst open with their pleasure.

Another favorite was a bathing picture that Daniel and I decided to recreate every weekend. During the week I spent hours in health food stores buying lavender soap, loofa sponges, and an East Indian bubble elixir called Treasures of the Sea, whose beads turned the bath a hot blue like the turquoise waters of Daniel's island homeland. He brought volcanic pumice stone for my feet, his mother's homemade tropical shampoo for my hair, and coconut massage oil for my sunburned skin. Because he was deeply interested in geology, he made a life-size topographical map of my body, naming his favorite places—my back, hands, and neck—after mountains and valleys he'd studied on maps of the ancient world. I wrote him primitive poetry, reciting it in our bath as we faced each other, encircled by candles. In our glowing water cave, we were two initiates, learning the luxurious language of touch and time.

Some weekends studying our pillow book, we'd play my Miriam Makeba album, with its African drumming, or listen to recordings of Tibetan chants. We didn't understand the words, just the rhythm. It flowed through our bodies—drum with our heartbeats, chants with our breath. The music moved our hands as we slowly caressed each other. One night I washed Daniel's feet with my hair; another night he washed my hair and stroked it one hundred times, each stroke a prayer murmured for me. Another night, as we embraced, we imagined we were snakes in a slow-motion dance under the earth; in our play we were all the animals we loved, making love. And in our animal selves we glimpsed that this intimacy was a prayer for the whole Earth.

Sometimes we'd sit naked, back to back, like the pillow book illustrated, and simply breathe together. I could feel his heartbeat through my backbone, and I trembled to hear his pulse in my body. Then, turning face to face, we let waves of energy wash over us, and our bellies rose and fell together like molten lava. Each time Daniel felt himself on the edge of orgasm, we'd both keep still, our bodies against one another. Daniel discovered, quite by accident, that he could stop the urge to ejaculate by pressing on a sensitive point between his scrotum and anus for several seconds. This pressure would only increase his pleasure, allowing him to build wave after arousing wave. Instinctively, I would place my hand on top of his head, the other on his buttocks. It was like holding the whole of him between my hands. After a moment, we'd both grow calm and tenderly draw away from the fire in our genitals.

"Breathe, breathe," we'd say, and inhale in sync. The energy moved to our heads and feet all at once like an ecstatic undertow, a sensual, slow flow that awakened arms, tingled in legs, and sang along our spines. "Bottom of the ocean" we called this joy, as our bodies tumbled together, sinking deep, settling at last on the seabed where the pulse of something greater like the sea rocked us. Our skin smelled salty, and our naked bodies gleamed like phosphorescent fishes. We gave off our own light, our own spinning gravity. Sometimes I'd fall asleep, my body stretched on top of Daniel; sometimes I'd wake to find him resting atop me like a comforter made of soft skin. Even when we were apart during the day, we'd carry one another's bodies against our own like a fragrance, sweet and spicy.

It is a great irony of my youth that Daniel and I parted before I obtained the birth control pills to allow us *actual* intercourse. But in all our erotic explorations, we hardly missed "going all the way," since we had found so many other pleasurable ways. Only years later, after much spiritual exploration, did I recognize those months with Daniel as an intuitive blend of tantra, Taoist, and kundalini partner yoga. Daniel and I were very sad to part when he left school to study with a local guru. Mourning him, I finally got the pill, my own little compact wheel-of-life, and I lost my virginity then with a young man who was kind but less inspired than Daniel. But I consider Daniel my first lover; even without intercourse or procreation, we made something alive and holy between us. We made love.

Recently I was taken back to the sensual world I shared with Daniel when I began looking in used bookstores for a pillow book to give as a wedding present to my beloved agent and her fiancé. When I told a friend about my search, she responded, "What I'm putting on the pillows of my two teenage daughters these days aren't how-to's, but how-*not*-to's—I mean, AIDS pamphlets."

My friend, a single parent, was deeply concerned. "Having teenagers gives me nightmares," she told me. "Here my girls are supposed to be awakening to the mysteries and pleasures of their bodies; instead they have to reckon with a fatal disease. What do I tell my nineteen-year-old when she says, 'To make love now is to make death, isn't it, Mom?' "

The fears of my friend and her daughter are understandable. In the '90s, to lose one's virginity can also be to lose one's life. But as AIDS sets boundaries and limits on our sexuality, maybe we need to respond to the danger of intercourse not by closing ourselves off from each other but by exploring other ways of making love, by seeking a new Eros in this time of epidemic. I am not an authority on sex—in fact, I consider myself a pilgrim on my meandering, often bewildered way—but as a writer and bodyworker I'm becoming increasingly aware that our sexual stories are getting narrower and more limited while our imaginations are dominated by the fear of this modern plague. If we open ourselves to other ways of looking at sex, might we find alternatives to the terror?

Even those of us who do not face a high risk of AIDS can benefit from creating new sexual stories. For instance, my generation was at the front lines of the sexual revolution, armed with our birth control mandalas. Few of us remained virgins for long. Yet I have come to feel that another kind of virginity has remained intact for many of us who were '60s teens: the virgin territory of touch. What we did not realize about our sexual freedom was that we had much to lose—not physically, but emotionally—once we had the power to go from A to Z in a single night. In our rush to reach the genitals and intercourse, we take the straight and narrow freeway and miss the astonishing, lavish countryside of the body itself. We hurriedly pass on through territory that is wide open, awaiting our touch: the curves of calf and shoulder, the sculpted glory of low backs, the insides of thighs, the lovely flanks and forearms and fingers, the lips like the bright flesh of silken petals, so sensitive and telling.

Then there is the deep soul-searching of long, moving embrace, our bodies entwined and growing together like trees. In one of her 1985 advice columns, Ann Landers asked women this question: "Would you be content to be held close and treated tenderly and forget about 'the act'?" Within four days, she received 100,000 replies. Seventy-two percent said yes, they would be content simply being held, and of those respondents 40 percent were women under forty years old. I suspect that if this same question were asked of young men, a surprising number would agree that being sensually and tenderly held is oftentimes preferable to intercourse. In the recent anthology *To Be a Man: In Search of the Deep Masculine*, bodyworker Don Hanlon Johnson lamented the loneliness of the male body and the masculine ideal of standing alone: "Alone, we ache for contact. That ache, we now know from various medical studies, is a major factor in male patterns of illness, addiction, and death."

Might we add AIDS to that lonely list of killers? Recent scientific studies show that the AIDS virus survives our cures because it can easily change and mutate new forms; we might outwit AIDS by following the same strategy—changing our ways in order to survive. What if we had sex with fewer partners and touched each other more? It is our loss of sensuality's life force, our focus on sex instead of intimacy, and our forgetting to truly touch another body and soul that has contributed to the spread of sexually transmitted diseases. A massage therapist friend of mine who volunteers for In Touch, a Seattle organization of licensed therapists devoted to massaging people with AIDS, tells me, "Often my clients weep and say I know their bodies better than any lover, that I've touched them more often than anyone in their lives."

The current widespread interest in therapeutic massage and other bodywork techniques may well be an effort to teach ourselves how to touch and be touched, to learn forms of physical expression that have to do with the whole body, play, and trust rather than the genitals, orgasm, and danger. If we teach ourselves and our children skillful, conscious touch, we might find a healing—not only from the AIDS epidemic, but also from the inner wounds that come from living in a culture in which sexuality has silenced much of our native sensuality. It is not enough anymore to pass out condoms and AIDS education brochures or preach impossible abstinence. Young and mature alike, we all deserve enlightened education that includes specific sensual techniques and alternatives to intercourse.

Here are a few lessons we might consider teaching ourselves and then our young.

COMPASSION: TOUCHING WITH LOVE

In describing her healing ministry with lepers in India, Mother Teresa has said, "We must touch with love." Her words embody a truth that much of modern touch has forgotten: that compassion (literally, "to suffer with") can be part of the essential gift exchange we offer each other's bodies. Many of us have experienced, when touching a body broken or in pain, that we feel an actual movement in our hearts—an echoing ache, an opening, as if our bodies resonate with another's anguish. It is a physical reaction, body to body, as our hands sense the other's agony. And in response, our hands soothe, hold, embrace, massage, memorize.

Elisabeth Kübler-Ross, M.D., tells this story of her early medical training: There was a hospital aide who was a favorite of the patients, and every time she visited a room the patient's vital signs would pick up and the person would seem remarkably improved or at least out of pain. No one on the hospital staff paid much mind to this woman's restorative visits until Kübler-Ross took her aside and asked, "What are you doing to the patients when you visit?" At first the aide was afraid of reprimand and wouldn't answer, but finally, her confidence won, the woman said simply, "I touch them. I just touch them."

If we were to teach compassionate touch as part of our sex education courses, wouldn't lovemaking become a truly healing encounter? If instead of denying the specter of AIDS in our sex lives we were to face it fully by admitting our terror—of intimacy, of death—might we be more able to touch one another with kind, conscious hands? Might we make sexual contracts that we don't break, knowing that we literally hold another's life in our hands? Might this new compassion for another's body inspire honesty and profound trust? A mindful preliminary to intercourse, then, would be getting an AIDS test together. This is certainly a prerequisite for understanding sex as compassion.

A bisexual friend of mine who has been practicing safe sex for almost a decade went with his new girlfriend to the clinic for their tests. Both were terrified; they held hands in the waiting room, and after their tests they had a long, romantic dinner at which they talked about all their previous partners, their fears of the future, their hopes. During dinner, my friend realized that this was the first time he'd really felt himself participating in a conscious initiation rite before choosing a sexual partner.

"I looked at my girlfriend across the table," he said. "She was scared, yet open as I was, and I thought, We're crossing a *threshold* together like in those ancient mystery traditions. We're undergoing a test; we're looking into our own souls and each other's eyes like some mirror. Something will be revealed to us. We'll be changed."

His girlfriend gazed at him and took his hand tenderly. "I feel so sorry for us," she said with a sigh. "What if we find out we're infected: What if only one of us has AIDS? Will we still want to touch each other?"

For a long moment they were both very quiet. Then the girlfriend said, "I would still touch you. I would find a way to touch you that wouldn't hurt either of us."

As it turned out, it was the girlfriend who tested positive, and my friend has been devotedly by her side throughout her long sickness. As a couple, they've educated themselves in compassionate touch, each learning massage to share with the other. Many of my friend's gay male friends have led the way in helping his girlfriend face her future.

Recently my friend commented that when he lies down beside his girlfriend they both imagine that their embrace is a physical prayer for our species—our bewildered brokenhearted species. "We cry a lot together," he said. "We cry for ourselves and for everybody who loves us and for *every body*."

A compassion that begins with learning how to touch each other without doing harm is a lesson we could all learn at an early age. The various religious organizations could participate in this training by teaching their own stories—not of hellfire, shame, and denial of the flesh but of the sacredness of our bodies. For the sake of our children, Christian preachers would focus not on the crucifixion but on many other scenes from Christ's life, such as Mary Magdalene, his most beloved disciple, washing his weary feet with the soft luxury of her scented hair. One of the few radiant memories of my Southern childhood spent among fundamentalists is of watching a backwoods congregation practice the rite of foot-washing. Old men bent down on creaking knees to bathe the calloused, aching feet of ancient women; boys and girls bent over one another's dusty feet, their faces rapt, utterly attentive as if those lowly, unwashed soles were indeed souls.

Many other world religions also have healing traditions—from the Chinese Taoist masters to the Native American shamans. In fact, among Native American beliefs is the concept that when we are ill we have literally succumbed to a loss of soul—that the soul is wandering away from the body and cannot find a way back. The shaman, through the use of herbs and visions, journeys to the realm of the lost soul and calls that spirit back to the broken body. Compassion is a way of calling our souls back into our bodies and healing the terrible split that has wounded us within for thousands of years. Who knows what we can heal when we lay our hands on ourselves and each other in loving, mindful touch?

PRACTICING SELF LOVE

A massage therapist colleague recently told this story. She used to hate her hair. "It was thin and patchy," she said. "Every morning I'd glare at it in the mirror and demand to know why it was so ugly. One day during this daily cursing I touched my hair and it felt so . . . so sad, dejected. I suddenly understood that all my life I'd focused on my hair as my worst liability, blamed it. How could my hair grow under such contempt?"

The woman made a promise to herself. Every morning for a

month she'd brush her hair and sing to it, talk to it, tell it how beautiful it was. "Such loving kindness works on plants," she said. "Why not my hair?" After the month, she noticed that her hair had a new shine. She decided to continue this loving practice, and within a year her hair was no longer growing in patches but was thick and wavy—astonishing her hairdresser. "It's not Sophia Loren hair," my friend said shyly. "But it's . . . well, it's downright beautiful to me."

The new physics tells us that when we look at something, we change it by the simple act of observing. Because for so much of history, humans have viewed loving the body and exploring sexuality as sinful, doesn't it make sense that we would invoke self-hatred and despair every time we intimately touched ourselves or others? The real sin is not, as some religions might warn us, the "self-abuse" of touching our own bodies sexually; it is abusing the body by despising it. In the same way that my friend changed her hair from the inside out, we might teach ourselves self-love by choosing to honor whatever part of our body we have always disliked, by creating rituals and rites that celebrate that thigh or belly or buttocks that have borne so much of our contempt.

The same is true for our genitals. In her book *Masturbation, Tantra and Self Love*, Margo Woods describes the practice of self-love as a kind of meditation, as an "opening of the heart": "The most important thing to know about being with a partner is knowing how to be with yourself," Woods writes. "It is absolutely necessary to have a private sex life." When we open our body to another for sex, it's as though we are opening our home to share with that person. Our private acts of self-love can help instill in us a respect for our body that will prevent us from sharing our "home" with someone who would condemn or damage it. Our inner critics are always with us; all we can do is balance them with a tolerance for our own frailties, our inevitable shortcomings, our humanness. We are not perfect, but we are still, every one of us, holy.

TANTRA IN THIS TIME OF AIDS

For thousands of years, Tibetans, Indians, and Chinese have apprenticed themselves to the ancient sexual art of tantra by practicing lovemaking as a sacrament. According to this Hindu tradition, tantra was first embodied in the god Shiva and goddess Shakti, whose divine lovemaking was a dance that they believed kept the world spinning. In today's world, with the AIDS epidemic and other impediments to intimacy spinning out of control, this ancient tradition seems more relevant than ever.

In Sanskrit, the word *tantra* means "expansion" or "weaving." When we weave other ways of giving and receiving sexual energy—expanding our sensual repertoire to include everything from bathing to gazing to bodywork to prayer to playful dialogue—we are invoking this ancient tantric spirit.

In *The Art of Sexual Ecstasy*, author Margot Anand reminds us that tantric students were trained in many skills, "such as conversation, dance, ceremony, massage, flower arrangement, costumes and makeup, music, hygiene, breathing, and meditation." Tantric yoga was a partnership practice that focused on health as much as spiritual and sexual intimacy. The word *yoga* means to "join together" self with the sacred. In other words, tantra has long been known as a holistic approach toward union—of bodies, minds, and souls.

Today we need an intimacy that involves all our senses, our science, our healing, and our health. Turning to tantra in a time of AIDS is one way we can heal the spirit-mind-body split that has harmed our bodies for so many thousands of years. Studying tantra together can offer couples, whether first-time partners or longtime companions, a new definition of lovemaking.

Tantra is not always sexual—it is a realm of intimacy entered through conscious touch and reverence for another's body. At one end of the spectrum, you can practice tantra with a friend, giving and receiving nonsexual touch. With massage so widely available in so many varieties—from the gentle acupressure of *jin shin jyutsu* to the deep muscle work of Rolfing—we have a tremendous opportunity to explore one another's bodies through healing touch. Nonsexual touch can be a powerful life force and a physical communion. By learning to touch and teaching the skill to our children, we create a future in which we'll have a multitude of choices both during intimacy and in our everyday life. We open ourselves and our relationships to being touched by more people than simply our sexual partner. This, too, is tantra—the weaving of the nonsexual into territory that we previously only allowed our lovers.

Midway along the tantric spectrum is the art of sensual massage. Sexual arousal and intercourse are not the goals; the only goal is to feel, surrendering your skin to the slow caress of a partner. Take turns as giver and receiver of the pleasurable strokes—without acting upon the genital impulses that arise. Sometimes during tantric massage a person will sob; other times ecstasy will take you, shivering along your spine and limbs; other times it will be a quiet illumination, like the body meditating. To share tantra with a partner is to slow down and pay attention to the sometimes unloved parts of the body, such as that Cesarean scar that stretches across a rounded belly like a child's tattoo—"I was here!"

With practice and play, our hands can learn to listen to another's body as if hearing the most astonishing music: There is the pulse of the blood rivers running like rapids in our veins; the delicate wind chimes of the breath; the subtle energies of the nervous system that sing high and clear as a tuning force; and the *thrum-thrum* of the heartbeat, like a strong African drum, talking, telling stories from the vast interior of our bodies—these beautiful, forlorn bodies that are our true shelter, our home, our heaven.

At the more sexual end of the tantric spectrum are techniques including intercourse—such as ejaculation control, deep breathing, and varying positions—to increase pleasure *and* enlightenment. In *The Art of Sexual Ecstasy*, Anand writes that with tantric practice "the orgasmic sensations are no longer exclusively dependent on genital interaction but are often perceived as an altered state of consciousness."

Tantra also offers us another expansion in our sensual life: a healing of our sexual wounds. "You can't ask a therapist to heal you through touch," says Charles Muir, author with his wife, Caroline, of the book *Tantra: The Art of Conscious Loving*. "But your tantric partner can help you heal sexual wounds." The couple "makes the journey together," says Muir. Imagine asking your sexual partner to participate in your healing. For people who have been raped, suffered incest, or been in other ways abused, consciously involving one's sexual partner in the healing process is offering that person a gift of intimacy usually only shared by a therapist or the most trusted friend.

One of my friends, sexually abused by both brother and father, has been studying tantra with her husband for the past five years. They attended workshops and read texts, but the real healing has been in their learning conscious touch. "We use our imagination," she told me, then laughed. "We call it 'playing doctor,' those times we set up specifically for sexual healing. I begin by telling him a memory of what my brother or father did to me. He will listen, gently touching my leg or hand. Sometimes he cries with me; other times he lets me hit him with pillows. When it gets really bad, I just start growling and he lets me wrestle him to the ground and win ... *every time*. Other times he's my bodyguard and protects me." She pauses, then adds with deep feeling, "I have never been so grateful to any lover. And I'm grateful also to my body because it is beginning to forget the past and learn new and pleasurable responses to his touch. This is tantra, this is true union—I wouldn't exchange my husband for a hundred other lovers."

Another friend of mine who is midway in his AIDS journey told me that he's been to thirty-six funerals in the past year. "All my friends and lovers are dead," he says. "I can't get over mourning one before another dies. All I want to do is cry—cry for the rest of my life." He pauses. "Then there are other times; I remember how it felt to have so much life force in me, to burst with passion, to embrace another's body with a whoop and a holler and a hallelujah!"

He turns to his lover, a young man who recently found out he also is HIV-positive. "We had our first date the day I got my test results back," this man says. "AIDS puts everything in perspective. We didn't play any ambivalent games. We knew we had very little time left to love, and we wanted to learn all about each other, including our bodies." He stops, then continues in a very soft voice. "I have never made love before so deeply—it is a healing every time he touches me. It goes so deep."

"Yes," his partner adds quietly. "I may be dying, but I am also healing."

SEXUAL HEALING AND SACRED SENSUALITY

In ancient civilizations, such as Sumeria, Egypt, and Greece, sacred sex was a healing act. Those who returned from war were taken first to the temples of the Holy Prostitutes. Here the soldiers were restored to their sense of Self, after having seen so much bloodshed and violence and death. Each maiden in the society was asked to serve at least a day in this temple ritual. These women considered their service a sacred honoring of the goddess; it was a privilege to perform the holy arts of sexual healing. The priestess-prostitutes offered ritual bathing, cleansing, massaging, praying, and purification through lovemaking. This holy lovemaking restored health and balance so the soldier could return to daily life.

"The ancients knew what we've forgotten," writer and therapist Deena Metzger said in a recent television interview about the Holy Prostitutes. "Think what might have healed in our Vietnam veterans if they'd returned to society through the temples of the Holy Prostitute." Instead of restoration to the sensual life force, we have the sad statistic of having lost many Vietnam veterans to postwar suicides. Metzger believes that this ancient ritual was less about sex than about soul-making. In her essay "Revamping the World: On the Return of the Holy Prostitute" (*Utne Reader*, August/September 1985), she wrote, "Through the Holy Prostitute one came to God."

The ancients recognized sensuality as a life force strong enough to redeem the warrior from death's stranglehold. If we as a culture choose to restore the life wish to our sexuality and so balance the death wish that lurks new within our lovemaking, we could change our future. Sensual education can be as vital as sex education. If every couple were to make pillow books together, what new story might we write on the open book of our broken bodies?

Sexual healing is *the* healing of our times. Like those ancient soldiers surviving battlefields to return to the temple of the Holy Prostitutes and reenter the doorway to divine life here on Earth, we have all been through our own personal wars. We've all borne witness to terrors and violence. Too long has death been what declared us divine. Our religions have focused on it; our warrior myths celebrated it. We have seen so much death we are breeding it.

In his moving essay "Bodhi Is the Body" (from *The Erotic Impulse*), Marco Vassi writes: "To know oneself as a body is more important, at this moment in history, than to read the words of all the wise men who have ever lived." And to learn how to touch each other's bodies as if they were our hearts and souls, as if we can save our own lives, is the work and foreplay of the future.

THE ALL-HOURS
LULLABY SERVICE

For L. L. and D. G.

WHEN I WAS IN COLLEGE DURING THE LATE SIXTIES, there were so many reasons we couldn't sleep. There were sit-ins and love-ins, there were all-night study and primal scream sessions, there was the joy of sex and the angst of the Vietnam War, there were dream workshops and astral traveling—there was, in fact, everything that could be done politically, psychologically, and sexually lying down, except something very simple and vital: sleep.

At the University of California (at the Davis campus, where I fled after one of my friends was hospitalized, having been teargassed in the Berkeley library during Reagan's response to People's Park), I lived in the first co-ed dorm.

It was a difficult first year, with several suicides, many busts in this drug haven of a dormitory, and too many close encounters of the unkind, the untrained, the unknown. It, the unknown, stretched out, even for us jaded eighteen-year-olds, into brief futures. No one expected to live much past thirty; nuclear war or our own burnout would spare us the decrepitude, if not the wisdom, of old age. But I think more difficult for us than contemplating the end of the world, the war, was discovering that we were, after all, still very young and somehow still virgin. We knew so much about empathy, so little about intimacy.

So it was no wonder we couldn't sleep alone; and even after sex, we couldn't sleep together. Who could rest when the world was such a wreck? We could feel it turning, spinning, veering off course right under our beds—the big, broken world was our boogeyman.

One night one of us in the dorm was brave or innocent enough to look under his bed and meet that boogeyman. Antonio was a small fellow from a vast Italian family; before college he'd longed to be a priest. Now he was a pusher, and he was also crouched in the duck-and-cover position in the middle of his dorm room, catatonic; the needle on his stereo had stuck, playing over and over, "I am a rock, I am an iiiiiii. . . ."

My two friends and I were in the stairwell singing. We were very serious singers, having discovered that in all the swirl of this psychological experiment, we guinea pigs could raise our voices, not in protest or praise but in three-part harmony. We were distracted from our syncopated parts by Simon and Garfunkel astutter next door. All we heard was "aiiieee . . . aieeeee," which I've since learned are the syllables of lament in Greek. Aggrieved, we entered Antonio's room and found him a zombie.

His roommate was gone; she might have provided some clue to his condition. Had she just walked out on her would-be priest and now bunkmate? No, said someone wandering by stoned in the hallway. She'd gone to the health center with her encounter-group leader to get help. Meanwhile, there was nothing to do but wait.

It was odd that there was no ambulance, no one to take Antonio away, for surely he was in some extremity of pain or injury; we just couldn't see the wound. I don't exactly remember how it happened, whether we were bored—catatonics really don't capture the imagination after the initial shock—or being sympathetic, but we began to sing. Soon we were soaring. Our three-part harmony sounded perfect for once, even without the resonance of the stairwell. We slid into our beloved songs, the free range of our voices analagous to sailing together on the same boat, and we made our own wind.

During my grandfather's favorite lullaby, Antonio, though still gone, began to breathe in exact rhythm with us. It was like having a fourth part to the harmony. We included him like a very small child whose body isn't bellows or verbal enough to sing but is right alongside us. The lullaby went on forever. We were afraid if we stopped singing Antonio might go away again, even stop breathing, drown, man overboard.

As our lullaby finally faded, Antonio slowly hunched his back, stretched his arms out before him as if in some yoga posture, and then glanced up at us, bewildered. "Sorry," he said, still not quite all in residence, "I guess I got stuck."

"So was your record," was all we could think to say before his roommate returned with the nurse from the health center.

"Overdose?" asked the nurse with a certain weariness. "Astral traveling? Bad trip?"

"I think he just needed to sleep," said Antonio's girlfriend softly. "We haven't had much lately." She looked so tired, the dark and deep skin beneath her eyes like bruises.

"Please come back," Antonio told us as the nurse took him away. "Come back and sing to me."

Antonio did not come back to our dorm. We never heard what happened to him. Perhaps he is a priest somewhere, or a rock, or an island. But we kept singing that year. Word got out that we would come sing lullabies to those on bad trips. Soon we were getting calls almost every night. Eight floors of freaked-out freshmen kept us so busy that we actually started charging ten dollars a singing session. We got tagged the All-Hours and Insomniacs' Lullaby Service. We sang to bulimics to keep them from throwing up; we sang to anorexics while they forced food; we sang to students whom Quaaludes kept awake; we sang to those recovering from the latest encounter sessions; and we sang to all our peers who had been touched, felt, politicized, feminized, militarized—everything but harmonized.

Lullabies have a way of washing over the body and soul like a loving mammy's hand giving a bath, except on the inside. And for the singers it is also a comfort. Singing alongside someone who knows where your voice will go by the arch of an eyebrow, the slight crease of concentration in the lips, this being known and being present together without talk, without touch, with only the ebb and flow of harmony like Möbius strips of sound eternally moving in and out of the body with the breath—this is how I finally began to learn about intimacy.

My partners in that long-ago lullaby service still call cross-country; we don't talk much. We sing on the phone and send tapes back and forth. As my friends' voices play on the cassette, I again hear the harmonies come in my head like insights, like memories, and like all the years ahead now that we've survived into our forties. I have even begun to consider that it is perhaps a good time to bring back the All-Hours and Insomniacs' Lullaby Service.

Today we sing lullabies to our babies, but rarely to ourselves or one another. But I think perhaps now we veterans of the sixties might truly begin to sing lullabies together for all those years we sang protest songs and were so afraid of the world, of the boogeyman. They say children grow in their sleep. Perhaps now as grown-ups we need someone to sing us lullabies because even though we are adults, we haven't stopped growing. But like Antonio's wound, or like lullabies, all that grows in us is now on the inside and often in the dark.

STUFF AS DREAMS
ARE MADE ON

THE FIRST TIME I BELIEVED THAT DREAM LIFE MIGHT
be as important as daily life was the year we lived on the
beach of the Atlantic Ocean and a dream saved my brother's
life. I was seven and shared a bedroom with my baby
brother. At night, radiators steaming, ocean waves as intimate and steady as our own breathing, I'd lie in my little bed,
one arm stretched out through the wooden bars of my
brother's crib. In rhythm to a lullaby my grandfather had inherited from his mammy and passed along to me, I'd sing and
pat my brother's small back like a miniature island across
which both our dreams would soon stretch out and enter into
some vast ocean of sleep.

> Sail, baby, sail
> Out across the sea
> Only don't forget to sail
> Back again to me

I'd sing, pat that sweetly powdered back, and we'd both
tack off into the night wind.

But one night my brother drifted too far. Of course, I was far away, too. I was in a dream that took much of its realistic detail from the Revere Beach amusement park we passed every day on our way to school in that rundown suburb of Boston. In the dream was the same cockamamie roller coaster, the submarine sandwich stand where we always squandered our allowances, and the Big Tent.

The Big Tent was really big; in fact, it looked like an amphitheater. And I was even smaller than a child. I was more the size of my infant brother. In my dream I flew straight into this Big Tent, not bothering with a ticket; even in a dream it seemed this was the wrong thing to do. A carnival barker called, "Everyone with tickets can leave," and the crowd stampeded out. I soon saw why: A giant fat lady, kind of like a King Kong in pink tights and red polka-dot panties, crashed into the Big Tent, making right for me. I gazed up and saw the ceiling was now a wide, polka-dot whiteness descending, and I screamed until I couldn't breathe. Down, down came the bottom, and then I was snuffed out, suffocated by spacious, spotted silk.

My screams summoned my father, who was immediately beside my bed. But then he started screaming, too. He threw my robe toward me; it thwacked the air, its plaid wool wrapping around my head, mummylike. I couldn't hear what Father was yelling—something about ice and the baby basin we used to give my brother baths. Barefooted, I ran for the ice and basin, returning to find my father holding my brother aloft. The baby was blue, naked, stretched flat and rigid; he was no longer a body but a board with familiar bumps.

Father laid my brother in the basin and packed him in three trays of ice. To this day I cannot hear the sound of champagne bottles in a bucket without wincing, because that was the sound of my brother's body convulsing under ice.

"Make your hand into a lobster claw," my father ordered,

and then he used my fingers like pincers to pull my brother's tongue out, holding it tightly. It felt like the time I'd unshelled a snail and been horrified to see that wobbly creature so very vulnerable without his hard, outer sheath; it hurt me to look at it for long.

But I could not help looking at my brother's body. He jerked with so much power I knew then that we must be more than a physical presence. For what moved through him, and by connection us, could only be called a great current. The only thing I'd ever felt as powerful as my baby brother's energy was a West Coast undertow that once took me until I breathed water. I had not died in the Pacific Ocean undertow, nor did my brother from his sudden high fever's convulsion.

But the doctor said he would have died within minutes had it not been for my nightmare that woke Father.

"What did you dream, anyway?" the doctor asked as he laid a supple, still sleeping baby back in the crib. My brother was no longer blue; he even cooed in his sleep like a mourning dove.

"I dreamed the fat lady sat down on me," I said.

"You were suffocating, then?" the doctor asked in a calm voice. "Well, so was your brother." Then he explained about babies and swallowing tongues.

I didn't like all the details. I tuned the doctor out and went back to sleep, only to find the Big Tent waiting for me. But this time I climbed up a chair as high as a mountain. As the fat lady moved to sit down on me again, I yelled up to her. She noticed me as she might a gnat, but she didn't sit down. Instead she leaned over, and her face, as big as a planet, loomed. Then she was laughing, crossing her tree-trunk arms as she waited for me to explain myself. I wasn't afraid anymore, but I also didn't know how to talk to the fat lady with her way up there and me way down on my wooden plateau. So we both simply waited, one for the other.

For years the Big Tent and fat lady waited for me. Every October around the date of my brother's long-ago fever, I used to have the same nightmare.

From the age of seven and that life-saving dream, I've developed the habit of asking myself questions before I go to bed at night, hoping my dreams might answer. Once I asked a dreamy question about a potential lover and was told by a brusque dream friend, who vaguely resembled my biology teacher, Mrs. Chopsky, that I needed new socks because mine were so thick my feet didn't touch ground. Of course, Mrs. Chopsky was right—love, or the longing for it, had ungrounded me so that my dreams had to step right in and be more realistic.

Recently, after many years' absence, the fat lady visited me again in my dreams. This time she was out of costume, out of the Big Tent. In fact, she was no longer the cartoon that my fear had first made of her. She was fully present, and, even though I was still smaller, I met her. I cannot say yet that I am comfortable with her, even in my dreams. I tell myself often that I am too small for the big picture, perhaps the Big Tent. But she will wait for me as she always has.

She waits for me the way I am learning to wait for myself before I take those conscious plunges into my unconscious depths, my own dreams. She waits for me much the way that the Atlantic Ocean waited all during long New England winters for us children to again enter her commanding waves, mindful of the undertow.

And when I think of dreaming, I believe that my dreams live alongside my daily life the way that ocean moved right across the busy street from our apartment house. We lived as children on the edge of infinity; we live as adults on the edge of our dreams. Perhaps we don't need any other vessel to go where we need to go. With sleep as our ship, we can sail, we can sail.

POWER IN THE BLOOD

Grant Paradise to be the womb . . . and Eden the placenta.
—Gnostic teacher Simon Magus,
as quoted by Hippolytus, REF. 6.14,
cited by Elaine Pagels in *The Gnostic Gospels*

O<small>N A BLITHE SPRING AFTERNOON IN THE LATE</small> 1970s, I sat with my little sister in an East Coast women's clinic gazing at an obscure black-and-white photo of her unborn child. In the ultrasound, her baby was the size of a tadpole. We didn't say a word; we'd already gone round and round for days. Father deserted, mother barely making it, how would she support this new life?

At last my sister said simply, "I just can't do it . . . But," my sister continued soberly, "what will happen to this baby if I don't?"

I opened my mouth to begin the bargaining, the advising, the begging—can you bring this child into a life unsupported? But instead I fell absolutely still as nausea swept over me—the way I'd felt when I found myself pregnant seven years before, a baby my body mercifully miscarried. "I couldn't forgive myself," my little sister was saying, calling me back to her.

My sister did not have an abortion. The child I first saw as a tadpole is now fifteen; he has two other siblings. And my sister spends much of her time in pro-life activism.

When my sister began her pro-life campaigning, I wondered, Who were the pro-lifers she had joined? Were they all housewives and mothers stripped of the prestige they once had as professional women? Because the world so little honored them as mothers, did they have to elevate motherhood to a sacrament and the choice against it to a sacrilege?

What I felt most from my sister, beneath her crusading, was fear. Of whom? Of what? And then one day, when she and I were talking about our inherited family fear of flying, I understood only too well. Our brother, whom we believe immune from our phobia because he hurls himself straight into it with his career as a navy aviator, was gently lecturing his three older sisters. He concluded simply, "When you get on a plane, just put yourself in God's hands."

We responded to our brother's logic with resigned silence. How could he know? The men in our family practically live on planes; the women stay below, bearing children, writing stories, and watching the sky with fear and trembling. Why? Is it something deeper than just a family phobia? Could it be that our feminine fear of the sky is an ancient terror? What came from the sky to frighten us, to make us as women so wary of leaving the Earth?

"How many women pilots in the navy, little brother?" my middle sister asked. When my brother balked, she said, "I guess we'll all be in that sky of yours soon enough."

And then I felt it: the fear. It's a smell, something hidden that sets free its scent, sweet and festering. Then I wondered if the Fundamentalists who picket abortion clinics are driven by the same fear I felt in my fundamentalist childhood. For when a fundamentalist woman faces those others who, like me, contemplate entering the doors of an abortion clinic, does she really see her sisters? Who she faces is her God. And He finds her sorely lacking.

This God lives in the sky, not on the Earth. He is God the

Father, without God the Mother. He has an only son; He has no daughters. And it is this masculine God that fundamentalist children are taught to fear. So why not also fear the sky where this God dwells—where our brother and father, but not mother or sisters, are welcome?

Though we were not arguing abortion that day, it was the first time I realized how profoundly this fundamentalist fear haunts many pro-life women. And it told me that, at core, abortion is a spiritual issue with two sides who are not speaking the same language. How can a woman carrying the sign JE-SUS HEARS THEIR TINY SCREAMS converse with another whose sign states ABORTION—EVERY WOMAN'S BIRTHRIGHT? It's like a screaming match between two tribes who offend each other simply because they occupy the same territory—in this case, a woman's body. To the pro-choice advocates, their fundamentalist sisters might as well be speaking in tongues; and to the pro-life true believers, their sisters are denying them dialogue on the only real issue—and that's not women, it's God.

Since my own pro-life sister is family, I search for some common language. Is there any place we meet? Is there any translation so that both sides can at least stop and understand each other, even identify some common ground? My personal journey to understand my sister and myself takes me first to family history and then to feminine history itself.

I used to think I could leave my fundamentalist fears in childhood, but I know now they will always be with me at some level, just as I will always feel uneasy when I step onto an airplane. I often remember: we three stair-step sisters, legs dangling in a pew, our shoulders hunched over as if awaiting a blow. The preacher shouts: *It was you who killed Him, sister, and me, brother, and every man, woman, child born. We killed Him. We surely did. We hung Him up on that cross where we all shoulda been.*

"Yes," my middle sister murmurs as I tell her this memory. "We're just born murderers."

Then I remember: pro-life marchers with their plastic baby dolls strung up on coat hangers, those small bodies splashed with painted blood. Tiny crucifixions. How did the fetus come to replace Christ on the cross?

"I'm sick of blood and crosses," I blurt to my sister, feeling slightly blasphemous. "Women are bleeding, too. I did, you did."

This sister, also a nurse and mother of three, found out during her fourth pregnancy that she carried a dead fetus. During the D & C, the gynecologist punctured her uterus, then rushed her to the hospital, where he proceeded to puncture her bladder. She survived to become pregnant a fifth time, though any pregnancy for her is now life-threatening. With her fifth pregnancy she suffered a miscarriage. She bled for a week, quietly going about her days as if this were not the death of a child, the end of her childbearing. "It's so hard," she'd said. "I love bringing babies into the world. I'm *good* at it."

Now on the phone she says softly, "Yes, there is a lot of women's blood in our family."

"Power in the blood!" I aim for black humor but instead feel sad as I quote the Baptist hymn that summons again our childhood:

> Would you be free of your burden of sin?
> There's power, power, wonder-working power
> In the precious blood of the Lamb.

The Lamb in this hymn is not a fetus, it is Christ bleeding on the cross. Anyone who understands fundamentalism in this country knows that this is a religion steeped in the Old Testament God. Christ is sacrifice and savior, but rarely can those paradoxical New Testament parables compete with the worldly, familiar fury of Jehovah. Christ, by comparison, seems downright feminine, unworldly. Had Christ been a divine daughter, forswearing the sword, the enigma of such a presence might have been better understood, during that ancient time as well as now.

But the feminine in Jehovah's Son is still unrecognized, just as the feminine counterpart of Jehovah is missing.

Is it any coincidence, then, that this more feminine New Testament Christ is also absent from those pro-life crosses? When did bloody fetuses usurp Christ's sacrifice? Do fetuses fulfill His role—to bring redemption and forgiveness? Do the pro-life women carry their own crosses because their role as mother is the only salvation God the Father allows them? If these women made themselves in Jehovah's image, wouldn't they be the *first* to understand sacrificing a child because sacrificial death in the New Testament brings eternal life?

To understand myself and my own pro-life sister, I've begun searching for answers to all these questions on the abortion issue, which so haunts my family. I wondered: When did all this power and blood and rebirth come together in our religion? Recently, there has appeared a well-documented body of scholarship on the ancient cultures whose spiritual life was centered in rites of biological motherhood and the Earth as feminine Goddess—Gaia, as the Greeks named her. Today, this Gaia-centered principle is reemerging in fields such as ecology—the Gaia theory that our Earth is a living, self-regulating organism—and religious rites that integrate this primordial feminine deity.

Important research such as Marija Gimbutas's archaeological excavations and study of what she calls "Goddess cultures" in prehistoric European civilizations explores the phenomenon of peaceful Upper Paleolithic and Neolithic cultures (6500–3500 B.C.). The heirs of these Great Mother civilizations are found in the Aegean, Mediterranean, and particularly the Minoan culture of Crete in the second millennium B.C. Gimbutas discovered, "There are no depictions of arms (weapons used against other humans) in any Paleolithic cave paintings. Archaeological evidence of hordes of brutal cavemen just does not exist. There are no remains of weapons used by man against man, no signs of groups of humans being slaughtered." Richard Leakey's research also defines early humans of several million years ago as peaceful and cooperative. These cultures are noted for their flexibility, their egalitarianism, the strong bonds between mothers and children. This was our way of life until about 3000 B.C., with the advent of the Bronze Age and the warrior tribes, with their weapons and their dominating Sky God.

If blood and power didn't first come together in warfare, when were they originally synonymous? In women's blood—and not just the blood of birth. Power was in women's blood from the beginning. The first method we had of telling time was by women's cycles: twenty-eight days between menstruations, twenty-eight days of the Moon's cycle. It was with reverence that our early ancestors greeted their own moon time; it was also with holy ceremony. The Moon was said herself to be "menstruating" as she fulfilled her fertile course, from waxing fullness to waning death to rebirth. Time was not then linear, unrelated, masculine—the minute-to-minute we have today so perfectly symbolized by the digital watch. Everything was in relationship to the circle, the whole. And in the center of this cycle were the Great Mother deities in sync with the Earth's seasons.

Blood rites were originally powerful transformation mysteries. Menstrual blood was sacred, symbolic of the woman's and the Earth's reproductive power. That power, like nature herself, was experienced as both life giving *and* death giving. In those days it was not the God of Genesis but the Great Mother who "giveth and taketh away" and whose name was nevertheless blessed. The root of the word *ritual* is *ritu* or rite, which originally referred to ancient public menstrual practices. For our ancestors, crossing the threshold from girlhood to womanhood was dramatic and awe inspiring. The wonder of it all: a body bleeds, cleanses, and is reborn. A body does not bleed for nine full moons and so gives birth to another body. How powerful and mysterious, then, this women's blood. Accumulated, it was the essence of creating new life. No wonder this blood was saved, used to fertilize crops, and precious drops offered in only the most important ceremonies.

The Old Testament lamb that was ritually sacrificed was in imitation of these first menstrual rites. Jehovah borrowed power from the feminine blood to make His own ceremonies, just as the male initiation rite of infant or adolescent circumcision cuts a boy's penis to imitate menstruation. How the blessing and power of those early Great Mother cultures' blood became the feminine "curse" and the masculine warfare (blood-shedding) myths of the Old Testament is important. But what is more important is that today we scrutinize the myths we live by to understand our own actions.

The word *hysteria* has its root in the word *womb*; the word *testament* in the word *testicle*, or "male witness." *Hysteria* is now used by psychology to describe dysfunction; *testament* is considered a sacred covenant "between God and man." Thus, the testicles can tell the truth; the womb lies. The truth as told in the Old Testament is that God, without female mate, created man, who then gave birth to woman from his own body. This is biologically backward from all we know or experience—yet, it is truth, testament. And in a masculine culture, of course, it will be law.

If a woman's womb lies and she is hysterical, isn't it then assumed that she can no more judge who lives and who dies? Is it surprising that she shuts herself off from the company of other equally "hysterical" women and spends her moon time alone, hiding the signs of her cyclical blood, which is no longer powerful and numinous but cursed?

Several summers ago I spent my first night in a moon lodge. In the Native American tradition, these menstrual huts, the forerunners of masculine sweat lodges, were shelters for feminine cleansing and meditation. A woman's moon time was considered a heightened period of spiritual insight, which the women brought back to benefit the tribe. The women were not outcast; they were in communion. They were not unclean; they were sanctified. Our moon lodge was made by midwives of bowed willow, red cloth, and earth. It looked like a womb, which we entered crawling on our hands and knees. Inside, lit by candles, the moon lodge was a luminous embrace of silken, scarlet membrane. It was small but spacious. We five women sat cross-legged and murmured, sang, or fell silent all night. When we spoke, it was to tell stories.

A midwife, mother of four, began. "My mother warned me about wantonness by telling me about Grandmother Amanda. She's my namesake, and we both share the same birthday. There's a portrait of her that I inherited—a young woman in white robes clings to a granite cross, wild waves everywhere, and the inscription: 'Our Dear Mother, Amanda, 1906, 30 years, 4 months, 4 days.' "

We were all quiet, candles glowing as if in memoriam these many years later. Above us, through the tepeelike opening, shone a full June Moon. There was the sweet smell of honeysuckle mixed with the medicinal scent of mugwort and other herbs we used for pain, for cleansing.

The midwife's face was dark, indistinct. I remember her hands, slender and strong. These were hands that welcomed newborns and stroked a mother's back bent in labor. For fifteen years this midwife had greeted over 500 babies. Now, she continued, "My Grandmother Amanda died of an abortion. She was thirty and had five children already. When her husband found Grandmother Amanda bleeding, he called the doctor, who rode out on his horse. But when the doctor recognized the abortive wound, he turned on his heels and walked away. 'She deserves it,' he told my grandfather. 'It's God's punishment for what she's done.' "

The midwife was still, then at last continued. "As a child, I felt haunted by my grandma Amanda. That picture of her hanging on a cross . . . that '4 months, 4 days' . . . I thought it was a code for how long she'd been pregnant. Later, when I traveled to Japan for my own illegal abortion, I sat in that strange hotel, holding pillows to my belly and sobbing. I imagined I talked to my unborn child and to Grandmother Amanda. I rocked and rocked. All night after the abortion, my older sister sat with me and held me as I bent double over those pillows. I was fifteen, and I understood everything."

Power in the blood—power and terrible knowledge. The knowledge of life and death and responsibility. As I sat listening, I realized these stories weren't the "old wives' tales" we've been warned against. They were old wise tales of women who, like the Great Mother, made the most profound choice we humans have—to give and to take life. This birth-death wisdom is born of woman, even in the Old Testament. For Eve is the first to taste of the Tree of Knowledge. And from this ancient, serpent-inspired knowledge comes mortality. It is as if the Hebrew God had to acknowledge and then punish the women for their encompassing both life and death.

The image of a woman hanging on a cross, a bloody woman at that, is blasphemous to a believer in the Old Testament God. But Christ's function in the New Testament is feminine: to reenact the blood rites, the cycle of birth, death, and rebirth. For without blood there cannot be birth—this much of our human biology survived the Old Testament censorship.

Perhaps those women who follow an Old Testament God have not yet integrated the feminine Christ. They seem stuck not in a cycle of birth, death, and rebirth but in death. Every time these women contemplate the act of abortion, they see it as a separate, unrelated act of female (therefore unsanctioned) judgment. The religion under which these women labor is based on an Old Testament in which Christ is all potential, *unborn*. To the pro-life mind, it is the blood of this unborn, wounded Messiah-child, instead of the female body's natural blood, that is shed every time a woman chooses abortion. Every time pro-choice women speak of their rights, what seems to get translated through this Old Testament myth is only the right to kill the unborn. Thus, sacrificial death is not linked by a healing feminine cycle to rebirth. This lifelong mothering cycle is irrelevant to a religion riveted on the death myth of crucifixion.

To the pro-life fundamentalists, the ultimate drama is not played out in picket lines or even courts. It takes place in the spiritual passion play of the Devil versus God. Because the drama, like Jehovah, is outside and beyond us, the focus on earthly matters is of scant importance. Perhaps this is why most fundamentalists are not typically moved by social reform issues such as nuclear disarmament or the environment.

Innocence, for fundamentalists, is lost at birth. Once you're born, you're bad. Bad as the Earth herself after the Fall. In medieval paintings, the world was depicted as the Devil's excrement. Into this dung pile comes the spiritually pure child— God's divine seed. Throughout the Middle Ages and into the Renaissance, it was believed that every drop of male semen contained a miniature, unseen fetus. The woman was God's vessel, to hold His holy seed until it was born. As passive receptacle, the woman's body, like the Earth, was meant to be abandoned, transcended, shed—the way a spiritual seedling must shatter and cast off its worthless shell. Not until 1827, with the scientific discovery of the ovum, was this myth of male seed as the divine source of all life itself shattered. It became biologically obvious that the female had her equal share of divine spark.

But society always lags behind science. Today, a woman's body is still not raised up by our mainstream religions as divine or sacred unless she is pregnant, her body a dwelling place for the holy male seed. Once the woman's body is emptied of the fetus, that potential Christ-child, the woman returns to her natural state, which, like that of the Earth, is of the Devil. The part of the woman's body that is not of the Devil is her womb. A womb is invisible, a spiritual temple within which a man can worship because it holds and nurtures the seed that will perpetuate him, his name. If, during this blessed gestation, a fetus has its separate soul, does that soul also need God's forgiveness for being human? Why does the Catholic church baptize a baby at birth and not at conception?

I suspect there is an official Catholic dictum to answer this question, though my Catholic friends cannot find answers in their catechism. In fact, it was Pope Innocent XI who in 1679 overturned a ban on abortion, allowing it before "quickening" (when the fetus is first felt by the mother) and stating that abortion is not murder because "the fetus lacks a rational soul and begins first to have one when it is born." And St. Thomas Aquinas, the thirteenth-century thinker, pinpointed "ensoulment"—the moment a fetus becomes human—at exactly forty days after conception for males and eighty days after conception for females. The longer gestation of a female soul says volumes about the church's meager estimation of women. But the more unusual point of these papal and patriarchal pronouncements is that fetal gestation was not then the battleground it is today.

Perhaps gestation is spared many of the church's rituals of sin and redemption because it is still perceived as a biological Garden of Eden. It is possible then that pro-life women see the decision to abort as a reenactment of the fall, for into this gestative Garden enters the snake. In pre-Christian cultures, the snake symbolized feminine wisdom. It is this snake who counsels a woman to exercise her Great Mother power of giving death, as well as life. Ancient depictions of the Goddess show her encircled with snakes like resplendent bracelets. And there are some archaeologists who speculate that the original Garden of Eden existed in the peaceful centuries of Goddess culture.

In our culture, still dominated by the masculine myth of war, the act of killing presupposes an enemy. In the older cultures, the taking of an unborn child's life, like Christ's crucifixion, was seen as a sacrifice, which in its original Latin means "to make sacred." As French scholar Ginette Paris observes in *Pagan Meditations*: "One aborts an impossible love, not a hatred." Primitive tribeswomen today still speak to the spirits of their unborn children before performing their ritual abortions. After the act, the woman is received by her tribal sisters and comforted in her grief, her loss, her choice.

As I sat in that moon lodge that summer, I wondered what might have happened if long ago when my sister and I sat in that women's clinic we might have been embraced by a united society of women welcoming us into the hard mysteries of life and death. What if nowadays the tribes of women outside abortion clinics were there not to bar entrance but rather to comfort and acknowledge a feminine sacrament? What if women's clinics were not based only on the masculine medical model of disease and surgical procedure but also on feminine healing? Why not a moon lodge near every abortion clinic, where a tribe of women meditate and comfort their own in the darkest phase of a woman's moon?

It is interesting to note that nowhere in the Old Testament does Jehovah actually forbid abortion, as He so specifically does acts such as false worship, adultery, and lying. Jehovah concerns Himself more with rules for masculine sexuality. He punishes Onan with death for spilling his seed on the Earth to prevent his brother's wife from conceiving. The prohibition against onanism, or male masturbation, which wastes God's seed, was the theological base for many of the later laws against contraception, homosexuality, and abortion.

The Old Testament myth is still very much with us. In 1988, *Newsweek* reported that one out of every six women in this country who has an abortion describes herself as an "evangelical Christian." And throughout the developing world, where American aid for family planning evangelically extends our fundamentalist stigma against abortion, a woman dies from a self-inflicted abortion every three minutes.

If it is only God the Father who "giveth and taketh away," if it is only God the Father who can sacrifice His own child because "God so loved the world"; if it is only God the Father who can sacrifice and redeem a child—then what can God the Mother do? She can give birth, and she can sacrifice herself for her child.

That summer night as I sat in the moon lodge, I longed for my little sister. But I doubt if she would ever accompany me to that red hut of women. Still, there might be some common ground.

"Sometimes the smallest things can bring us together," a younger woman in our moon lodge commented. "Like the women I work with. There's five of us in a department headed by a man. Well, we women aren't all close friends, but somehow we pretty much always know when we each start our periods. And because our boss would be embarrassed by such women's talk and we work in an open office, one of us came up with a rather subversive idea: On the first day of her period, she'd wear her elegant little Moon necklace. That gave me the idea of putting my favorite Picasso postcard—you know, the Cubist style of that woman's face split in half and kind of weird, wacked out?—up on my desk to let everyone know: *Back off!* Soon every one of us had a talisman for her moon time. Another co-worker always wore her red silk blouse; another woman bought herself flowers for her desk. She told our boss they were from her boyfriend. Do you think he ever noticed that those flowers came every month on the full Moon? We wondered, because without any word from us and probably without knowing what hit him, that guy went out and bought himself a watch with the phases of the Moon on it. Very expensive, that watch. But considering the money we saved him, by acknowledging and working within our natural rhythms, it might have been a bargain!"

In the moon lodge we all laughed, listening to crickets down by the lake. Bull frogs chimed in with their sonorous seesaw chorus. The Moon gleaming into our hut was so bright that someone asked, "Anyone know Moon stories?"

The midwife told us first of Artemis/Diana, goddess of wisdom, the hunt, the Moon, and childbirth. Her mother, Leto, gave birth to Zeus's twins—Artemis and Apollo. Artemis's birth was completely painless; she turned and midwifed her mother during Apollo's dangerous, difficult birth. It was to Artemis, the midwife told us, that women cried out in childbirth pain or ecstasy. As goddess of the hunt, Artemis also sacrificed the animals she loved—and this destructive element in her nature was in perfect sync with her role as bringer of children into the world.

As the midwife told more stories of feminine deities—the gnostic Sophia, who, like the Egyptian Isis and Babylonian Ishtar/Inanna, descended to the underworld to find wisdom and rebirth (and often to save her masculine counterpart), the Chinese Buddhist Kuan Yin, all-compassionate and wise—I remembered my great-grandmother's wedding ring. It is mine now—this antique, very delicate cameo of Artemis.

My great-grandmother did not pass down to her daughter the feminine secrets of birth, death, fertility. The goddess of the hunt, a masculine myth, survived proudly in my family's storytelling. But what became of Artemis's midwifery and feminine secrets?

About the time my great-grandmother was accepting her wedding ring, the role of women as midwives was becoming increasingly unacceptable. Up until the mid-1800s, abortion in this country was legal. The movement to stop the midwives and "granny women" or "yarb doctors," as they were called in the South, was spearheaded by a fledgling American Medical Association campaigning against abortion practitioners. The tradition of midwives was economically competitive, not to mention undermining to a doctor's authority. Again, we have a male priesthood repressing women's traditional societies and secrets in true Old Testament style.

A God who will have no others before Him. A God who does not share and, in fact, steals power from the feminine. A God without a partner. What does this God do with daughters? He declares war on the Devil through their bodies, and the women, in turn, declare war on themselves, their sisters.

But what if, instead of warring with our sisters, women found another way?

"I would like to dedicate this moon lodge in the name of my two sisters, my great-grandmother, hunter and midwife, and my own mother," I said to the other women surrounding me. It was almost light. We were luxuriously sleepy; there was much blood shed among us. And with all the squatting, storytelling, and herbs, our cramps were gone. What was left was a trancelike contentment—for we'd shared a rite of passage long overdue us.

We turned to the midwife to lead us in an old chant:

> I am the daughter of the ancient Mother
> I am the daughter of the Mother of the world.
> O Inanna, O Inanna
> It is you who teaches us
> To die, be reborn, and rise again.

Then she said, "There are so many stories we could tell that women have told for thousands of years."

She reminded us of the Eleusinian mysteries of Demeter and Persephone. For centuries those mystery religions gave ancients hope of rebirth by participating in Mother Demeter's search to reunite with her daughter Persephone, queen of the Underworld, who brings the new life of spring back to a barren winter world. Another woman sang a chant to Isis, who helps us heal by lovingly re-membering her dismembered masculine mate, Osiris. An older woman, a professor, invoked *gnosis kardias*, the "way of the knowing heart," by calling on Sophia. At last the youngest woman told this recent story: On the day the first man walked on the Moon, a woman archaeologist discovered the ancient, lost Temple of Aphrodite, goddess of love and the Moon. Dolphins accompanied that archaeologist to the buried site in Turkey. Her story didn't make the newspapers, of course, for many years. It was a man's conquest of the Moon, not a woman's rediscovery of reverence for that Moon, that made headlines. "But rediscovery never belongs to the past," the young woman said firmly. "It belongs to the present and the future. It's what we make of it, once we discover it again."

At dawn we decided to tell a last story, the Navajo myth of Spider Grandmother. She is the smallest of the small, the greatest of the great. It was seemingly unimportant Spider Grandmother who brought light to her people after all the warriors had failed to capture the Sun. Spider Grandmother simply spun a small web to carry a bit of the Sun back to her tribe. I believe that night in our moon lodge we five women telling our small stories spun a web to bring some Moon light back to our own little tribes.

"Know the male," instructs the illustrious *Tao Te Ching*, "but keep to the female." For thousands of years, women and men have earnestly apprenticed themselves to "know the male." But many women have discovered that this is not the same as the feminine Delphic oracle "Know thyself." This most famous Delphic wisdom of knowing ourselves means that we all, male and female, must know our own feminine mysteries, and our Earth.

That night in the moon lodge I learned something about myself that had always mystified me. My moon, my first blood, began on the day of our school's big 6,000-yard walk-run. When I ran that dreaded race, I suddenly had so much power, I flew around the track. Never before or since have I won any footrace. And why, on the original day of menstruation? That night in the moon lodge, I learned that Changing Woman, called White Bead Woman, on her holy day of first menstruation, also ran a race. That is why the Navajos call a girl's first menstruation her "first race." She is given gifts because she has passed a threshold into her own power and mystery. Since that moon lodge night, I've made it a practice to buy myself a gift on the first day of my monthly moon—a small, and now not always private celebration.

I would like to give my own and all pro-life sisters a gift, too. But I must give them something they can accept. They cannot accept women in moon lodges. They have their own traditions. What I can give my own sister is something that I cannot buy. It is a gift exchange more difficult because it requires that I suspend my own beliefs and try to understand, if not embrace hers. What can I give my sister, then, in this attempt at understanding?

In contemplating the tradition that motivates her pro-life advocacy, I must acknowledge and allow my sister her very real pain about my own belief in legalized abortion.

The mistake pro-choice advocates make is engaging in this passion play of self-proclaimed holy war from a defensive or offensive posture. Instead, we might stand back from the fray and gaze upon this Warrior God-inspired movement as if it were simply the last gasp of patriarchal Christianity. This does

that we will refrain from legal lobbying in behalf of
means simply that we must *not* engage in the warfare
against our sisters. It means gazing at them across

the picket lines with compassion and nonviolent *gnosis*. We must act not from the fear and anger that belong to the old masculine testament but from our own feminine, knowing hearts. This understanding is a right that can never be lost or legalized.

Some of us who are pro-choice are in much the same situation as conscientious objectors were during the world wars. Nor do we want to counter these fundamentalists with an evangelicalism of our own. Fear, anger, and self-righteousness make zealots, and even Christ refused to be a zealot. Warrior ways and thinking lead to battle.

How can I declare war on my own sister? She is not my enemy. She is my own blood. And blood is sacred. If I engage in a war, my sister and I will dehumanize each other so terribly that we'll forget we are from the same family.

What about finally finding the feminine way of power to balance our masculine ritual of *logos* (i.e., court trials, the flesh or word made legislation)? What about remembering that a woman's bloodletting can be natural, in keeping with the Earth's cycle? And finally, what about holding up to those driven by the Old Testament God the balance of a Christ who offered the seemingly impossible "Love your enemies"?

I propose to pitch my moon lodge a distance from all the abortion battle lines. There I'll share stories with my sisters rather than attack or defend myself from them. Running across the lines our daughters could be bearing gifts on the first days of our moons, no matter what our politics. With my small society of friends, I'll continue to chart our reproductive rhythms, a way of keeping time that is again timely. Knowing my body's temperature and reproductive cycle is a right no one can take away from me. And I'll continue to explore the feminine myths that have everyday meaning for me and my tribe. There are also teachings in every spiritual tradition, from Chinese Taoism to American Indian, celebrating sexual mysteries of conscious creation. There are women's secret societies that teach traditional remedies, herbs, rituals, and meditations to control and increase fertility. All these feminine ways of knowing ourselves may well be invaluable in a world bent on restricting our modern medical abortion procedures. There is so much to remember, to put back together of this feminine that has been so fragmented and forgotten.

If I had a daughter, when it came time to celebrate her rite of feminine passage, I would offer to take her to a moon lodge. There, in the company of witnessing women, we'd tell our stories and old wise tales of what it is to embody the blood and power of the feminine. No matter what the laws dictate, no matter how the abortion war might rage, there will also be these private nights of tribal, feminine knowing. There will be moon lodges pitched beyond the battlefields. Within them we will welcome and remember and give rebirth to an old and new myth. And there, we can teach our daughters, while the Moon shines on their brave womanliness, a meditation on the rite of abortion that we made the night of my first moon lodge:

> I approach this abortion as a sacred act of compassion
> and letting go.
> Many mothers before me, in grief and with wisdom, have
> made holy this sacrifice.
> What I do is sorrowful and I seek succor, from my Great
> Mother and Father.
> I ask for their divine presence.
> Be near me; comfort and hold me.
> I commit this responsible act because I believe that the
> world, not the womb, is the true Garden.
> Because I believe birth is a celebration, not a damnation.
> It is a time of original orgasm, not original sin.
> When I do decide to give birth, it will be a promise of life-
> long mothering love.

I now ask for the spirit of this, my child, to come again—
when the world and when I welcome its rebirth.

It was the women who took Christ down off that cross. Spirit may have abandoned His broken body, but the women did not. In a small, unheroic act, they carried Christ like a child back to the Earth's womb, back to the Great Mother, to be born again. It was to Mary Magdalene, His earthly companion, that Christ first chose to reveal his resurrection.

Can we now, these thousands of years later, allow ourselves, like Christ, to receive the forgiving embrace of the feminine? Then we can take ourselves down off that old, rugged cross and accept the strong, balancing arms of God the Mother—She, who also gives and takes life, She who calls our fundamentalist sisters back from their Old Testament fall, into their knowing hearts, their full, fearless power.

Sisters of the Road

My aunts are a wild lot. Ozark born and back-woods bred, Aunts Nettie Mae, Mary Leola, and Donna Ruth explain their electric spirits by saying, "We got a touch of the tarbrush and a touch of the tepee in our blood. That makes our family just plain touched."

Most summers of my childhood were spent in the wayward company of these aunts, who provided a perfect counterpoint to my father's (their brother's) pretense of normalcy and practical calm. "Cutups," my aunts called themselves. To this day it is their greatest delight to aim potshots, if not punches, at the "balloon heads that pass for menfolk in our family."

This summer, at a biyearly family reunion in northern Georgia, hosted by Aunt Mary Leola, my aunts pushed my father into the motel swimming pool right in the middle of one of his "lecture series," as Nettie Mae dryly describes my father's penchant for impromptu pontificating.

"Listen to your daddy, you gals," she mugged behind his back, before shoving him unceremoniously into the water. "He's the world's expert on everything!"

If there were any experts in my family's tribe, they were

my rambunctious aunts. Like imprinted ducklings, my two sisters and I used to tag after our aunts—smoking as they did in the piny woods, dancing to the 1950s bebop, and defying my parents' stern religion with so much laughter that we were lamented by my mother as "born-again backslid."

Our aunts not only tolerated my sisters' and my gawky devotion, they embraced it. "We never had no time or money for no doll babies," Aunt Mary Leola explained in her deep, tobacco-rough voice. "You young'uns were our toys. We got some of our childhood back when we played with you gals."

My aunts' and father's childhood was marked by poverty, not play. Nettie Mae tells the story of the one pair of shoes she and my father shared; they went to school on alternate days, depending on whose turn it was to wear the shoes and walk the ten miles to a country schoolhouse. Nevertheless, my father won the state spelling bee when he was in third grade, and Nettie Mae was known for her shrewdness at numbers and reading. The oldest of the five farm children, Nettie Mae was married young to a full-blooded Cherokee who, as Donna Ruth likes to say, "adores her so much, Nettie Mae might as well be his whole tribe."

As children, my sisters and I were afraid of this taciturn Uncle George; his humor was black and beyond us. Now, he's a favorite uncle, a man to be counted on to demonstrate how to treat a lady. Last reunion, we sat spellbound as Uncle George packed Nettie Mae's suitcase, his masculine paws perfectly folding our aunt's negligee like holy raiment. We'd always seen my mother packing my father's suitcase for his frequent business trips. But Uncle George's tenderness with his wife's underwear, the exact way he folded the pleats in her pedal pushers, the bright cotton socks he handled so deftly, as if juggling warm popovers, made us realize that none of our boyfriends and husbands had ever folded our laundry, much less packed our suitcases.

"It's a revelation to these gals, Nettie Mae," Donna Ruth joked, poking her husband's ribs. "Now, my Bill here, I have to stay on top of him every minute or he might turn right back into a male chauvinist pig!"

"Suuuu-weeee . . . ," my aunts yodeled in unison.

Donna Ruth's fifth husband, Bill, is a Lutheran minister whose sense of humor matches his wife's. "How else would I survive these sisters of hers?" he laughs. "A man either laughs with them or they're on off down the road."

Off down the road might well be a one-way trip cross-country. There is a tradition in my father's family of criss-crossing the continent in family caravans, like reunions on the road. To travel with my aunts and all my cousins was to be part of a chain of vans, pickups, and U-Hauls that stopped and circled at night in a wagon train of family. We still take over entire motels. When Grandaddy died, all fifty of us piled into an Ozark motel. After crying our eyes out for two days, we decided to play practical jokes on one another—hiding cars, dousing one another from balconies with water balloons, and generally raising hell by way of a wake. My sister remarked that we'd done Grandaddy proud because we "figured out how to put the *fun* back into funeral."

After the funeral, caravans took off every which way. My sisters and I, along with Cousin Doug, continued our road reunion through the South—from the Ozarks to Memphis to Atlanta to Miami.

It was Cousin Doug who gave us the supreme compliment. "You girls have taken over where our aunts left off."

He was referring to the "rebels-of-the-road" way we sisters now travel, a direct inheritance from Nettie Mae, Donna Ruth, and Mary Leola. It isn't that we're so open-minded. My younger sister—whom we call Marla Mosby after Colonel John S. Mosby, the Confederate Gray Ghost who terrorized Yankees—is "wild in the wrong direction," as my sister Paula

("Pooh") gleefully explains. Riding in Mosby's van, complete with shag rug and VCR in the back for her three boys, was for me like riding around inside my political opponent's point of view.

Last summer's family reunion saw yet another series of sisters on the road. The moment I arrived in north Georgia, Aunts Mary Leola and Donna Ruth swept me up between them for a ride into the backcountry in Mary Leola's red pickup truck. Her husband, Lloyd, had recently died, leaving Mary not much more than her sixty-two infertile acres and farmhouse. All four of her children live within fifteen minutes' drive of Mary Leola, and they share tending to their mother's land and needs. Mary Leola raises peacocks "so stupid I had to buy me some little roosters to teach 'em not to fall into their drinking water and eat their food instead of stare at it while starving." She also has a day job, which "runs her ragged."

Sitting between my aunts as we roared over red ruts in the Georgia backwoods, Mary Leola smoking Pall Malls and Donna Ruth telling family jokes, I couldn't help but notice the gearshift grinding between my thighs.

"Aunt Mary," I protested, "can't you shift without goosing me?"

"Ahhhh, honey." She howled. "You've had worse!"

At that my aunts screamed with laughter and almost missed stopping for a garage sale at which I bought a tape recorder for five bucks and Aunt Mary Leola bought me a hand-crocheted, button-on red-yarn collar. I also bought my father a birthday belt buckle with a bucking bronco on it for three dollars, and Donna Ruth purchased a country wildflower porcelain vase. Then it was back on the road, radio blaring country and western as we three sang along at the top of our voices.

My ex-brother-in-law called our multigenerational sisters-of-the-road legacy "Talk and Ride." "All you women do is talk and ride and sing," he complained on the few short trips he shared with my aunts or my sisters and me. My aunts also found a way to push him into the pool. A day later he was blithely pushed down a hill, video camera equipment banging all the way, to remind him that "only men who really *like* women are allowed here." As a final ritual, Aunt Mary Leola smeared chocolate frosting all over his face when he was found guilty of uttering a sexist statement. He fought back by dropping a pincer bug down Mary's "front porch," as she calls her ample bosom.

The day my sisters and I took off for our road trip through Georgia to the Florida Keys, Mary Leola settled next to me on a swing on my cousin Little Lloyd's wooden front porch and we rocked in the midday heat. Aunt Mary detailed for me the secret recipe for her beloved blackberry cobbler, then settled back in the swing, lit a cigarette, thoughtfully picked a slit of tobacco from her lip, and took up what we call her "storytelling song." Her deep voice dropped into a lulling, melodic chant.

"Brenda Sue, little sister, you see that house over yonder?"

"Yes'm."

"Use the family feeling and see what you git offn' that old place."

I closed my eyes and tuned in to the family ESP we all struggle to understand as another kind of evidence to be weighed with all the rest. "Well . . . violence and passion . . . maybe murder. Something feels real bad over there. . . ."

"Yes, indeed," Aunt Mary took up, nodding. For a moment it was as if we'd both fallen asleep in a wooden cradle that creaked and swung and stirred the only breeze. "Little Lloyd's wife's brother, Sam, was livin' there. He had this little gal come up right regular. They was real cozy until she stopped comin' round. Then one day, Little Lloyd sees her truck, figures they's done made up." Aunt Mary gave me a deep look. Her black eyes are hooded, her cheekbones high, her skin swarthy with the Seminole blood running strong in her veins. My immediate family are the only ones who don't show the Indian blood. "White people," the others call us; we've always felt somewhat ashamed of our fair skin, how we six stand out like a bright knot amidst dark, handsome faces in reunion photos.

"What'dya think happens next, darlin'?" Aunt Mary Leola fixed me with her ancient Indian eyes. It's what she's asked me all my life, as if the story were already told and we simply had to remember it, tap into its rhythms and rightness like tributaries finding their main stream.

"Someone dies."

"Oh, honey." Mary Leola nodded. "You *are* with me." She lit another cigarette, and smoke hung in the air like humidity. "Well, Little Lloyd decides after three days of not seeing hide nor hair of anybody—not Sam, not his girlfriend—to investigate. Little Lloyd walks into the house, helloing his head off. No answer. Sudden, he sees blood smeared everywhere—on the walls, on the TV set, the phone with its wires cut clean through. He starts in to shaking, but he's brave and goes deeper into that bloody house. There on the linoleum kitchen floor he finds Sam's little gal, lyin' flat and still. Lordy, that gal's got three eyes ... and the one in the middle is a bullet hole!"

The swing stopped, and Mary Leola stared straight at me. "Young'un, she'd been alyin' there three days and three nights just like sweet Jesus in the tomb."

"Did she live?" I demanded.

"Wouldn't call it no resurrection." Mary Leola sighed. "Sure, she's walkin' round now, draggin' an arm and a leg. Says she's got no memory a'tall of that night. I think she's just scared witless. Wouldn't you be? And Little Lloyd like to crack up at the sight of that gal shot smack between the eyes. Put him off his accounting numbers for some weeks. Then they done found that boy Sam ten days later. He was the major suspect until a fisherman seen him layin' up the crick back yonder. Sam was so disintegrated, there weren't nothin' left of him but a high school ring." Aunt Mary Leola turns to me, a hand slung around my shoulder. "Ain't that a mystery now? You tell *me* what happened, child."

I tried. I made up plots and subplots, and we swung higher until my sisters called me away.

We piled each set of their kids into two identical vans, revved for our continuing cross-country reunion.

"Y'all finish the story in the car, honey" is how Mary Leola says good-bye. "Carry my love along. Precious cargo." As we embraced, she added softly, "You take care your sisters, hear?

As my sisters, Pooh and Mosby, and I drove off, we weren't three miles out of town before we were on the CBs that make our Talk and Ride easy between vans. We sisters have our own frequency, tuned beneath the truckers with their dull delight in spotting Smokeys and good peach pie pit stops. On our CB frequency, we don't exchange facts; we take up our stories. As Pooh says, "Gossip is our path to the soul."

"What do you think of Aunt Mary's idea?" I asked Pooh in the lead car. Her handle is Pink Pistol. Mine is Rambling Ruby. "Want to all of us live together when we're old?"

"Sure thing, Ramble!" Pooh's voice crackled. "But I'm not going to cook anymore. We'll hire help, play killer Ping-Pong instead of shuffleboard, and we'll dance instead of do that stupid low-impact aerobics for ancients."

Mosby, riding shotgun with the Pink Pistol, took over the CB. "Roger, this is Gray Ghost . . . ." Behind her three children screamed to take their turn, and there were signs of a struggle over the microphone. Her sovereignty at last restored to the airwaves, Mosby said, "You know, I was working in this nursing home with these two old ladies, Miss Eula and Miss Louise. They'd never left Virginia in their ninety-odd years.

Sisters, they were. I overheard Miss Eula tell Miss Louise that their new doctor was no gentleman because he didn't wear his shirttail tucked in. Thing is, the poor guy was wearing scrubs! Anyway, Miss Eula said she guessed she had to forgive him because he was from Ethiopia. When Miss Louise asked, 'Where's Eeeetheeeoooopeeea?' Miss Eula said, 'Oh, honey, it's somewhere south there of Richmond.' "

"We won't make that mistake," I said. "Not with all our traveling."

"Not unless one of us is senile!" the Pink Pistol shouted into the CB.

"Hey, Ramble, you believe in euthanasia?"

"For my sisters, yes," I teased. "It might be self-defense if we all end up living together again."

The CB fell silent, static companionably crackling between the cars. Someone turned on the VCR behind my driver's seat, watching *The Little Mermaid* for the hundredth time. I look around at my two nieces and a nephew, who sang along with "Kiss the Girl"—every word perfect. One was learning harmony from listening to her mother and aunts on this caravan.

The night before I had told my nephews and nieces the continuing story we were all making up called "Bandito Bear." The youngest of three girls, Lissie, sobbed upon hearing that Bandito's great grizzly mother had died and left him starving. "Didn't Bandito Bear have *sistuhs*?" she wailed with her Southern accent, unable to imagine life without a sister-caretaker.

Fierce sisterhood, the habit of rebellion and true believers, runs strong in my family. Both of my grandmothers taught college during World War I, only to be replaced by men returning from war. One grandmother fell from the intellectual grace of teaching university astronomy courses to teaching kindergarten; the other descended deep into madness. But each passed along to her daughters a highly charged current of brilliance short-circuited. The next generation tenaciously took up the grandmothers' dropped torch and burned bright; my aunts formed their own feminine family to support their declared matriarchy. While marrying, they kept their compass on the True North of feminine rights and realms. I have never seen any of my aunts "kowtow to any man," as they put it. Nor have I seen them reverse the roles and "ride roughshod" over their men. They have simply let their husbands know that "I got sisters watching over me—and you." This last is said sweetly but with that inherited undercurrent that is so electric it is almost audible, the hiss of a snake, the sizzle of live wires.

There is a history in my family of sisters running away together. My aunts have all lived with one another when marriages went awry. Their future sisters' nursing home seems as pragmatic and shrewd as any other retirement plan. My mother didn't have sisters but quickly took up her in-laws' ways. She made a habit of running off to Southern Baptist conventions with her Women's Missionary Union sisters. In the early sixties, when women did not have the vote in her church, my mother and comrades commandeered the floor of the great convention hall in Virginia Beach and filibustered with all their feminine fury until the members allowed as women should be able to vote in their own churches.

My own sisters and I travel together at least once a year—and often we have planned these trips to heal broken hearts and homes. As my sister Pooh coolly remarks, "We've practiced leaving our husbands so many times, they know we mean business." Again, that slight crackling in the air.

The feminine electricity is like static on our sister CBs as we move down the highway. On this latest summer's sojourn, there was a deeper journey we three sisters took together. For the past decade my middle sister, Pooh, and I have been quietly aghast, guiltily united in our despair over our youngest sister Mosby's anti-abortion activism. Pooh, ever the mediator in our sibling bond, took the track of listening to Mosby and engaging with the Gray Ghost in political skirmishes. I, the eldest, simply dropped out of the dialogue and kept to the more tender track, mothering Mosby in the hope that she might feel our bond was deeper than our opposite beliefs. Of the two tactics, I must say Pooh's worked better over the years. Because she and Mosby were always in the fray, they were in constant communication. Unlike my frequent communion with Pooh on the phone, my intimacy with Mosby fell into ritual patterns— holidays, birthdays, emergencies.

So at a recent summer's reunion, with all three sisters and children traveling South together, there loomed potential disaster. As I climbed into Mosby's van, I noted her new bumper stickers, one reflecting her patriotism over the Persian Gulf, the other a modified version of her anti-abortion stand. SUPPORT OUR TROOPS declared the left side of her bumper; and, on the right, ABORTION STOPS A BEATING HEART was inscribed over the bright red medical zigzags of an EKG chart. My nephews happily informed me that they'd named their dog Patriot after the successful Patriot missile system; and my youngest nephew wore his Persian Gulf T-shirt on the trip. Since it was the Fourth of July, we stopped for fireworks in Stone Mountain, Georgia, where a laser program was beamed against the granite monolith carving of Jefferson Davis, Stonewall Jackson, and General Robert E. Lee. As a country singer intoned "Glory, glory, hallelujah" from "The Battle Hymn of the Republic," the fundamentalists and patriots in my family snapped to attention while I sat quietly eyeing fireflies. In the dark our phosphorescent headbands glowed orange and purple like halos.

"This must be hell on a liberal like you, sis!" My sister Mosby leaned over and laughed. "Don't think you're the ugly-duckling misfit, darling. You do belong in this family. We'd never let you go."

·   ·   ·

I don't ever want to be let go—as strange as my family is, as wild as my aunts are, as different as I am from my siblings, we grew from common ground. Later on down the road, as I was riding with Mosby, she turned to me and said softly, "Remember all those summer nights down on the Yellow River when we used to live here in Georgia? You and I sitting on the riverbanks, with our feet in the water and talking. I was in high school, you were home from college, and we told each other everything. We'd just moved and we were a mess. You thought you were going crazy with dizzy spells, and the doctor said it might be a brain tumor. . . ."

"Oh, those were the days. . . ." I made a face.

"It was a nightmare, sure." She fell silent. "But we could talk about it; we told each other we were wide awake in the middle of a bad dream. I thought if we could be close then, we'd get through anything."

"We have," I said. "We will."

"Politics ain't nothing compared to a nightmare," Mosby said.

We looked steadily at each other, she now in the driver's seat and me handing out pimento cheese sandwiches our aunts had packed us for the trip. Behind us, the children fought over their food. "I've still got my beliefs," Mosby said softly, "*and* my sisters."

There was that subtle electricity, then static on the CB as the Pink Pistol tuned in from her lead car. "Any y'all feel like a pit stop? There's peach cobbler down the road at Exit 212. Aunt Mary's cobbler didn't last a minute with these savages."

"Suuu-weeeee," we all sang between cars, between the seats, the states. "Sisters of the road!"

Much of what I first learned about wandering and being "bad enough to be yourself," as Aunt Mary Leola calls it, I learned from my aunts; most of what I learned about the lifelong journey of friendship I learned from my siblings. When we're all as old as Miss Eula and Miss Louise and in our own nursing home—perhaps we'll inherit it from Nettie Mae, Donna Ruth, and Mary Leola—our next generation will carry us, singing, as sisters take to the road.

Vaster Than Empires
and More Slow

Some midnight, midcontinent, streaking across Kansas in a honeymoon sleeper, my parents made me. My mother had recently retired at age twenty-one from her wartime years as a station telegrapher on the Wabash "Cannonball" line. In the toss-up between her railroading and marriage to a young forester, my father won. But not for long.

Though he took my mother away from her first steamy, steel love, he couldn't take trains from her blood. Riding the rails runs in our family like a dominant gene. Some families pass along sharpshooter eyes or stolid legs like roots—but my sisters and brother and I inherited a hobo waywardness.

In fact, our uncle *was* a hobo. Our earliest stories of my mother's brother, Clark, were of dropping him at a railroad crossing in the middle of a California desert. He knelt by the tracks as if in prayer. After a long while he leapt up, slung his knapsack and bedroll over his shoulder, and sprinted off. But where was the train? Uncle Clark counted aloud as he ran, shouting with what we children instantly recognized—though it was rare in adults—as sheer joy.

Suddenly the ground thundered, and, as if called, a train caught up with Uncle Clark. It slowed only a little, but not enough to be caught, even by my uncle, strong and sleek as he was. Undaunted, Uncle Clark let out a piercing whistle. Out of the black square shadow of one boxcar shot a long arm. In a flash my uncle grabbed it and was hoisted inside the wide door. We never saw the other hobos, we only heard them laughing at the show they'd given us townies.

Not too long after that, our parents yielded to their four children's clamor to take a cross-country train ride from California to St. Louis for the usual summer stint with our Ozarkian kin. The first night in our drawing room, my three-year-old sister frog-kicked my father out of the top berth and knocked Mother silly. Unperturbed by the hubbub above, my other sister, baby brother, and I played Parcheesi in the bottom berth. I remember most the horizons that gently curved both Earth and steel tracks as we rolled along. The world was wide and open—and so were we. We even endured my father's lectures on the changing flora and fauna.

"This used to be buffalo country," he'd say sadly as empty Midwest prairie swept by. We imagined shaggy ghosts grazing in the sweet grass. Sometimes Father would quiz us as if it weren't summer vacation at all. "Did you know, kids, that ninety-nine percent of this country's population lives on one percent of the land?"

Cities seemed so silly to us when we saw the vast green thrust of corn, the cows who kept chewing their cuds even as this iron leviathan shrieked alongside them. Such spaciousness, we decided, makes daydreamers of animals and people. We stared out the window at the cows, chewing our bubble gum, our eyes half-lidded. We'd even forget to blow bubbles. After all, our so-called Vista-Dome was already a cool, blue bubble.

Our family still takes trains cross-continent in this era of faxes and flight. Trains are a trance state that makes planes seem high-pitched, a hysteria. The human heart is slow. How, in the space of several hours, can we really adjust to opposing sides of a continent, or comprehend leave-taking, longing, loss, or even love?

Uncle Clark, who is now retired from Social Security, still vacations near narrow-gauge railroads, and many Sundays he reads the paper down at the local depot, counting trains and chatting with ex-Cannonball conductors. My sister Paula, her three girls, and I now consider the Silver Meteor line, which runs up and down the eastern seaboard from Miami to New York City, as our home away from home.

On these trips we've tallied up one madman, one car hit by our train, and one fatal heart attack. Because my sister is a surgical nurse, we're often in on the action. The cigar-smoking madman we named Mr. Neanderthal. He screamed at the conductor loud enough to make him turn over our sleeper to him because Amtrak had double-booked it; then Mr. Neanderthal barricaded himself inside. We rode most of the twenty-two hours in the dining car, with free wine and stories from the stewards. They reported that Mr. Neanderthal was in our ex-sleeper, clad in nothing but his skivvies, with a gun in one hand and an egg salad sandwich—presumably packed by Mrs. Neanderthal—in the other. He was threatening to buy Amtrak because he was so rich and so angry.

It was during the heart attack—the man was past help from Paula's CPR—that a conductor informed us, "No one ever dies on a train. They always die in the nearest city." He told us the story of an old couple traveling from Miami to Hoboken, New Jersey. For hours the stewards eyed this man, who never moved or spoke, his hat crunched down over his face. Yet his food disappeared, and his wife chatted with him. "But, you know, that guy was awful still," the conductor said. "Finally I approached the couple and said, 'Ma'am, is your husband all right?' She waved me off and said, 'He's *always* been quiet.'

"Well"—the conductor laughed—"that old guy wasn't quiet; he was dead. But when we tried to insist upon moving him and stopping the train so we could call the ambulance, his wife screamed bloody murder. Then she pleaded with me, 'Can't you just carry my husband on to Hoboken in baggage?' "

Several summers ago, Paula planned her greatest train trip to date—traveling from West Palm Beach cross-country to San Francisco, then up to Seattle, along the Canadian border, then back down to Florida. When my family heard about my sister's train adventure, we all signed up to join her on various jogs. Mother boarded and rode from DC to Philadelphia; and I flew to San Francisco to take the Coast Starlight train back to Seattle.

When I met my sister, her three girls, and their Colombian nanny in San Francisco, they had accumulated another friend, Madelyn, and her eight-year-old son and nineteen bags. "It's like traveling with the shah of Iran," I complained, as porters boarded us. We had booked two sleeper compartments in the same car. Over the next twenty-two hours we stretched ourselves, amoebalike, between observation car, dining car, and compartments.

As the Coast Starlight steamed out of the Bay Area, we cozily settled ourselves into the dining car. "Our sleeper car is a regular soap opera," Paula happily reported. "See that couple over there? They've been riding since Atlanta—and the honeymoon is definitely over!"

"What is it about trains that makes ordinary people into the cast of 'As the World Turns'?" I asked.

"It's the close quarters," my sister explained. "Over the days everyone becomes a kind of gypsy family living in one long house."

She proceeded to fill us in on the details of our traveling companions. There was a Swiss family whose son had attached himself to our troop because his parents were preoccupied with a murderous, never-ending Monopoly game. Then there was the old lady in Sleeper C of our car who monopolized our steward because she believed first-class meant servants. Later I visited this intriguing, if demanding woman and heard her tales of having survived both the 1906 and the 1989 San Francisco earthquakes. Seems railroading was in her blood, too. Her father was a conductor from Sparks, Nevada. Once he'd worked the legendary Olympian Hiawatha train, which once ran from Chicago to Seattle.

That first night the dining car was divine. As the adults lingered over elegant wine and peach pie, we sent the kids sprawling into the Vista-Dome, where they watched the movie *The Bear* on a big-screen TV. My nieces counted shooting stars like so many sparks thrown from the train. When we all finally retired to our tidy bunks, we were experts at the polite, lurching sidestep and shuffle of narrow aisles. Looking into each roomette as we slowly passed, I saw a man leaning over his needlepoint, an old couple nodding on each other's shoulders as they held hands, fast asleep; I peeked into another sleeper and eyed an entire family with attention riveted on their bleeping Game Boys and a teenage couple who might as well have been in the backseat at the drive-in. So much life right alongside mine.

As we all bunked down for the rockabye night, I figured we were somewhere between the redwoods and the northern California seacoast—wild land with only a few lights here and there. But inside this train was an intimacy, a tenderness as simple as sharing sleep. In our room's four bunks, we all hooked ourselves up to various headsets—everything from country and western to my own *Les Misérables* tape and my niece's "Sesame Street" songs. Lying happily in my berth, I gazed out the window at mountains silhouetted by a slight moon and gloried in the knowledge that this was how I chose to enter the world—by train.

Next morning during a breakfast of buttermilk hotcakes, sausage, and coffee, we stared down into chasms outside our window and hardly blinked as ancient Oregon forests surrounded us. Fog swirled as if the land were still asleep. We were at 5,000 feet outside Chemult, Oregon, when the mists cleared to reveal a mysterious, deep Odell Lake. The conductor told us in his leisurely travelogue that it is 300 feet deep. Staring down from the scant tracks we made as the Coast Starlight streaked across water, my niece insisted, "No, it's lots deeper. Something else lives there"—she looked at us, her expression at once wide-eyed and wise—"and it's not like us."

"Ohhhh, I don't know," my sister told her. "After a month on a train, what else *is* like us?"

She was right. I knew it, even after my mere sixteen-some hours. We were all changed. It wasn't the travel; it was the movement reflective of the stirring in our genes, our blood—all my mother's mesmerizing miles, all my uncle's hobo longings, all our own accumulated memories of just rocking along going somewhere, but not fast.

The way we travel reveals the way we live. I like delayed gratification; I like a lingering hand, a lulling voice, a close and deliberate dance. "As slow as molasses in January"—that's how my mother has always described taking trains. "Slow and sweet."

Already my sister and I are planning another summer's train trip. We rack up cross-country conference calls discussing the pros and cons of the Zephyr versus the Empire Builder. All winter we'll sort out which novels, clothes, games, and companions are just right for "the slow-motion adventure," as Paula calls our train rides. "Sometimes . . . ," she muses, as we talk long distance, "I think it takes almost as long to pack for a train trip as it does to take one."

We both laugh leisurely and fall silent. We've forgotten that there's a phone meter ticking away, we've forgotten all about expensive airwaves and the blank heavens above. We're thinking about buffalo ghosts in Kansas and a lake so deep there's nothing human about it. We might as well be lounging on our berths while something as slow and vast as a country drifts by us. Even cross-continent, we're on the same track, remembering all the sleepers that carried us, the steel that still vibrates in our blood, the great body that cradles us with long curves, with tunnels dark as dreams, with an unbroken embrace of Earth.

GIFT OF THE MAGI
CUPCAKES

In the South of my childhood, food and fellowship represented love. At Christmas there had to be an abundance or else we thought ourselves pitiful. I don't remember
Christmas presents so much as I do the food and presence of
certain people who have come to embody this holiday for me.

In those early days, grandparents abounded, and not only
grandparents but great-grandparents, two of whom I knew until I was almost ten. My great-grandmother Thomas was a
fierce but dreamy presence. Her wedding ring, which I inherited, was made for her by Great-grandfather; it is a dark
cameo of Diana, the goddess of the hunt, childbirth, and the
moon. Great-grandmother Thomas encompassed all three: She
shot the wild Christmas turkeys or ducks, she bore four quite
bold sons and a pensive daughter, and she had a way of looking at the world with a visionary clarity as if she saw people
and their inner landscapes revealed, but by moonlight.

One of the things Great-grandmother saw quite clearly was
that at Christmas there must be much celebration of miracles
and mysteries. That's why, to this day, her recipe for Christ-

mas chowchow has never been revealed, even by my grand-mother, who still makes this tongue-tingling relish do to turkey what salsa does to pale tortillas. Perhaps it was Great-grandmother Thomas who started our family tradition of making our own moccasins on Christmas Eve, out of whatever the men had shot and tanned during the year. To sneak around the house way past midnight on Christmas Eve in mooseskin moccasins with our own bright beadwork was, to us children, a way of meeting the grown-ups' penchant for mystery with a bit of our own.

My grandmother Elsie has continued her mother's Christmas traditions by making a divinity that arouses more religious feeling than do many Christmas pageants. Grandmother is mysterious about this recipe, too. It is a sugary-stiff, white-hard fudge, studded with Georgia black walnuts—those strangely bitter, smoky nuts that seemed like illegal aliens to us children, perhaps because of all the fuss about bringing them up from Georgia, as if smuggled over the border by odd Mrs. Phoebe, the only supplier of Georgia black walnuts we knew. The arrangements to pick up the nuts were clandestine: middle-of-the-night drop-off points and the burlap bag of black walnuts hidden more diligently than any of our Christmas presents. To open those hard-shelled nuts was a minor miracle itself: Father placed them under a plywood board and then ran over them repeatedly with the beat-up Buick station wagon.

That was Grandmother's divinity, the petite madeleine of my childhood Christmas. But it was not the only holiday sweet. Mother added her cherry and pineapple fudge, her peanut-butter fruitcake, homemade nougat, and caramel pop-corn balls, all served with eggnog or Russian tea. A heathen once brought bourbon balls to our home, and we had gobbled half a dozen apiece before Mother could swoop down on them and deliver them over to the fate of all liquor in our house—down the drain. As the bourbon balls gurgled in the newfangled garbage disposal, we children spun around the tree, tipsy.

Later the same evening we were bundled up to go out into the crystal cold of that Christmas Eve to witness a live nativity scene. In keeping with the spirits of that evening and the bourbon balls, we were awestruck at the sight of the teenage Mary appearing astride her lowly donkey and shyly approaching the little lean-to barn where awaited a shivering gaggle of angels, wise men, and shepherds. We were moved by this modern Mary who calmed herself by blowing incandescent pink veils with each breath and her bubble gum.

After that Christmas epiphany, bubble gum became a staple in our stockings, a little ritual that my Catholic friends, who usually cornered the market on Mother Mary, miracles, and other saints, had to envy. It had never occurred to us before seeing that live nativity that Mary, the mother of such an important baby, might have been frightened or felt alone at Christmas. In fact, anybody being frightened or alone at Christmas seemed incongruous to us—though the adults were always hauling us off to progressive holiday dinners with the "shut-ins," as we heard them described.

Progressive dinners proceed from house to house, potluck course to course, and at Christmas there was often caroling in between, say, the orgy of hors d'oeuvres and the Caesar salad. Not just the usual carols; we sang spriggets of that year's Christmas cantata.

One year we even got so bold as to take our taste treats and Christmas cantata to the great St. Elizabeth's mental institution up in Washington, DC. The cantata was called "Night of Miracles," and the treats were called Gift of the Magi Cupcakes: chocolate on chocolate on chocolate, kind of like the original sin of chocolates. Some of us sang that cantata with dark-stained lips from sampling what should have gone to the shut-ins.

The inmates gathered in a circle, all dolled up for our visit. They nodded and tapped feet like normal folk, and we decided they weren't mad at all. I suppose we expected to see people transformed into pigs like in the Bible or someone foaming at the mouth. But they all ate their cupcakes and clapped, just like a go-to-church audience. All, that is, except a very small and very old lady with two bright splotches of rouge that endeared her to me because of Mary of the Pink Veils. She, alone of all women, peeled her Gift of the Magi Cupcake with delicate, white lace gloves and then, smiling pretty as you please as we belted out the rousing chorus of "Night of Miracles," this little lady smashed her cupcake atop her head.

I was so startled I forgot to sing, and all the way home I pondered this mystery. Was she adorning herself with food the way children do or the way we'd seen old people in nursing homes practically wear our imported Christmas peaches? I'd seen old people peck and nod happily over those peaches that didn't require putting in teeth. Was that little lace lady happy, too? Or was that cupcake anointment her own personal miracle? When I asked my grandmother, she said what Great-grandmother Thomas might have said: that everyone has his or her own way of celebrating Christmas and all we had to do was be there to see it, like the shepherds, the angels, and those other assembled witnesses who watched by moonlight. Then Grandmother went back to stuffing the wild duck that, the next time I saw it, would be glazed on a Christmas platter, its innards filled with apples and onions.

Parsnips in brown sugar, crocks of homemade hominy, sweet potatoes, red cabbage slaw, some kind of guessing-game salad we call heavenly hash—it will all be there again this Christmas. My grandmother, at ninety, still cooks her mother's Christmas chowchow, and her divinity is already in the mail.

If Grandmother were here in my kitchen this Christmas, she would ask me whom I've fed or sung to, and what personal miracles I've witnessed. She would not ask me if I am happy;

happiness is another one of those things meant to be a mystery. Grandmother would ask only that on Christmas no one be hungry, or alone of all their kind—and no celebration be unseen.

THE EVIDENCE OF
THINGS SEEN

WHAT I WITNESSED ONE VERY EARLY CHRISTMAS MORN-
ing when I was seven has spoiled me for the rest of my life. Or,
at least if not spoiled, then certainly it has made me more a
stranger in the strange land of modern love..

That year my family made one of its many migrations—at
Christmas we take airplanes and cross-country trips the way
other people take Valium—to southern Missouri and the almost mythical small town of my grandparents. I say mythical
because for my family, who never lived any longer than two
years in the same place, my grandparents' small town held
the dignity of Real Life because it continued with a regular
and trustworthy ordinariness. We didn't see Grandmother and
Grandfather flying off the face of the Earth every other year or
so and landing in strange cities looking like little aliens who
talked funny, laughed in all the wrong places, and wore an-
klets and noisy pink snow pants when all the other girls were
wearing subtle woolens.

We had landed in Boston that year, my father on fellowship
at Harvard; he lived among the library shelves and Mother

traipsed around Boston looking in vain for a Southern Baptist church where the people didn't sing hymns slow with Yankee accents. For Christmas it was decided that we would travel to her home and find solace there for enduring a new year back in New England.

There are some years of our childhood that we remember in exact detail as if everything happens in some darkroom of the mind, each event developed indelibly. Memories of those particular years are like flash cards. What I saw that Christmas morning in my grandparents' small town is such a flash card—it was my first lesson in lovemaking.

In my grandparents' spacious gray house, the big people slept on the ground floor and we children braved the second story—"closer to God," Grandmother would say as she tucked us in, but we were not at all convinced. For one thing there was the attic door right smack dab in the bathroom and the obviously haunted North Room, where I, the oldest, had to sleep alone, as well as the South Room, which was all too intimate with the weeping willow that rasped against the roof. In between, and in the middle of the night, was that attic where I'd once seen a Yankee hiding, though my uncle swore it was just his old army outfit. We smelled trunks of rotting, before-our-time things in that attic and little creatures died there, as we could attest when Grandmother every so often swept and we saw stiff mice whisked away without funerals.

That Christmas we were quite concerned for Santa, who would have to enter our grandparents' house at its most dangerous peak—the attic. But we were not so afraid for Santa's safety that we would leave the attic door open in case he needed us to rescue him from that dread, dark place.

Besides, I was suspicious of Santa. I kept these heresies to myself and only discussed them with my classmate Peter. He was from Germany, an alien like myself, and I was assigned to teach him English after school. But what we really did was go to the beach and lie under a rowboat and play Sleeping Beauty. First he was the prince and woke me with a kiss, then I took my turn being that swashbuckling smoocher. Peter learned little English, but I learned a lot about what it felt like to have a warm, lithe body against mine, slow-dancing in the sand with the complete innocence of curiosity. Because he was from Europe, and had been schooled by a French governess, Mlle. Véronique, I believed Peter knew more about the world. When he told me that Santa was to adults what Sleeping Beauty and the Prince were to us—a pretend and playful presence—I took it on faith. What was more amazing and difficult to take on faith was Mlle. Véronique's suggestion that when big people made love they somehow entered one another's bodies in much the same mysterious and gift-giving way that Santa entered houses.

I could say that Christmas dawn when I stole downstairs from my haunted room to sit quietly on the cedar chest at the end of my grandparents' bed that I was really waiting for Santa not to appear. But what I was really waiting for was to watch what happened when big people made love.

My grandparents slept side-by-side in their big four-poster and the in-between, winter light over their white comforter made them look like those museum exhibits of woolly mammoths under the snow. Their faces as they slept were very pale, mouths open like baby birds, and I remember thinking how very young they looked in sleep, how expectant. I was expectant, too, and as the first sun slanted across their bed my grandfather gave a great kick just like a frog. Off went the covers! I fell back, horrified. I thought of Peter growing up into a Frog Prince and never turning back into the pretty little boy I loved to kiss. Maybe lovemaking changed people physically and they could not return to their right shape or form. I almost ran out of the room.

My grandparents lay near one another, their nightshirts wrapped around their spindly legs. Not touching, they slept soundly on their backs. I crept closer and saw that they breathed in perfect rhythm, their bellies rising and falling as if one breath moved through both their bodies. Then I, too, breathed deeply, now not at all afraid. I felt that somehow I was part of them—not between them or down at the end of the bed like the onlooker I had felt so much of my life. No, I felt *with* them as if that bed were one big body and we all fit just fine.

In my chest something moved and I felt more space inside my rib cage—a wide expanse that opened me from the inside out, not the way I'd seen adults crack open lobsters but the way I'd watched big people open their mouths slowly when they were touched and then bow their heads and say, for once, absolutely nothing.

At that moment my grandmother opened her mouth and tilted her head slightly upward as if to receive, and then she did something so right for her I knew this was Grandmother's way of making love. She cooed, a low, throbbing sound in her throat like the way she spoke to birds when feeding them old bread. My grandfather's head tilted back too, and he answered her with a warbling, sweet snore.

Mesmerized, I watched as two hands softly moved out in perfect sync to clasp across that wide bed—clasp and capture one another and hold still as if this were not sleep but constancy. This was how big people made love, made me.

This, I would later whisper to Peter when I woke him from his dream with a kiss, this was lovemaking: two hands finding one another at exactly the right time, even while sleeping. This I could believe in, the way I'd witnessed my grandparents' bodies believe in one another without seeing, by simply reaching out in the dark.

What I told my sisters and brother that morning when I

climbed the stairs was that Santa had come, though I, too, had passed through it in a dream. Because that morning when my grandparents awoke, they called me into their big bed and we three lay listening for Santa—who would always come to me, girlie, my grandfather said, even if I never saw him.

THE SACREDNESS
OF CHORES

For C.H.

ONE BRIGHT MAY MORNING, MY ARMS PILED HIGH WITH clean, freshly folded laundry, I walked up to my housemate and dear friend's room and discovered that she'd taken her life. Jo lay on that pale green carpet as if fallen from a great height, one hand outstretched. I did not see the gun gleaming like a dark fist at her temple as I knelt down to grab her wrist. Not dead, I thought, teeth chattering, just hurt. I had never seen anyone so hurt. Fumbling with her wrist, I finally felt a thready pulse against my forefinger—but it was only my own heart beating. I was so cold. Never have I felt that bone-deep shiver and chill. Her body was warm with sunlight, even though its own inner warmth was gone.

Then I saw her face, the eyelids darkly swollen, shut. From her nose and mouth ran congealed rushes of blood, a red so brilliant and dense that I remembered my sister saying that she'd once watched a heart explode on the operating table as she assisted a surgery, that it bloomed upward from the body like a rose bursting open. For a moment I jumped up, then fell right down, legs buckling. I again took Jo's hand, thinking somehow my touch might spare her the sight of herself.

But it was I who needed sparing. Alongside Jo's dead body, I knelt on all fours and howled until suddenly I heard a far-off accompaniment. It was a thud-thud, not of footsteps up the stairs but of something from deep within the bowels of the house itself. I listened, head cocked like an animal, listening with my eyes. And only after a time did I recognize the spin of the dryer. Then the thumping stopped and a piercing buzz began. It summoned me, this shrill signal, to stand upright, to leave the dead, to go downstairs and open the dryer door. More clean clothes tumbled into my arms, and I buried my face in the warm, fragrant cotton and colorful flannel. And because I could not carry Jo's body alone, because she no longer carried herself, I bunched her clean laundry against my chest and called for help. Kneeling on my hands and knees, I carefully folded every sock and cotton camisole, every blouse and nightgown until the sirens stopped at my door.

It was so breathtakingly swift, so complete, Jo's leave-taking of her body, of her son and family and friends; and, though in my mind some part of me will always be howling on all fours in fury and grief over her brutal abandonment, there also lingers with me these fourteen years later the exact weight and clean smell of her laundry.

After sharing domestic chores for six months, Jo and I had struck a bargain: I did laundry and vacuumed; she did dishes and dusting. We shared scouring bathrooms, cooking, and the yard work, which was a kind of desultory dance between dandelions and an ancient push mower that mangled more than it trimmed. On the afternoon of Jo's death, I found myself sitting absolutely still in the kitchen. I stared at the bright haze of sunlight off Lake Washington, the silly burble of my coffee cheerful on the stove, the whir of the fridge, its rhythm loud and labored. I thought of the food inside this stupid, square, and noisy box—*Let it all rot and die!* At the same moment I remembered dully, *I should defrost that fridge.* It had been on my list of chores for the day, right after the laundry.

My morning list for that May day had read:

1) Finish Chapter 10
2) Laundry
3) Defrost fridge
4) Meet P.N. in the Market (check for rhubarb)

I gazed at the little list, and it seemed so earnest, so busy, so foolish. What did defrosting fridges, making a strawberry-rhubarb pie, or even finishing a chapter have to do with anything when all the while I'd scribbled that list my friend had been dead upstairs? The coroner said she'd died deep in the night while I lay down the hall sleeping, practicing for my own death.

I looked despairingly down at my clothes and realized I was still in my pajamas, the ones I'd bought in imitation of Lauren Bacall, the ones I'd rolled up at wrist and ankle, the ones, I realized now, must also be washed clean. It was only when I threw my pajamas in the washer, slathered Cheer on the load, and turned on the churning machine that I found myself crying, kneeling on the cold cement floor and at last lamenting. It was safe enough to sob—the world had not stopped spinning, just as this washing machine spun and spun its little load through all its warm, delicate cycles.

This is how my friends found me. First, Paula, who arrived and busied herself during all the unexpected official paperwork of death by mowing the lawn furiously, up and down outside as if her precise patterns in the scraggly grass could bring order back to my little yard, my small world. Two days later, when I decided to leave this house, my friends Laura and Susan came heroically armed with buckets, Fantastik, and huge, brightly colored sponges to scrub and scour and spend hours on their hands and knees, a final cleansing of Jo's room, a kind of womanly worship. I put Alberta Hunter on the stereo, and we all got down on the floor, crying and cleaning. As we left the house for the last time, it shone in the sun, welcoming. Others would live here and wake up to the lapping lake, the coffee, fresh laundry. This house was again ready for life, life abundant.

Those mundane tasks that sunny May fourteen years ago have forever changed my sense of daily life. Those simple chores, both solitary and in the company of other women, were my first comfort in what was also my first death. The smell of Comet is forever linked with consolation, the spin of a dryer with survival, the syncopated chant of women scrubbing with the racial memory of reverence.

"Cleaning is incantation, physical prayer," says a friend who is an artist. "You create a small and ordered sacred place that has been touched a thousand times by your hands. It's a ritual of caring."

"The actual cleaning is sometimes secondary to the mental housekeeping that takes place," adds my friend Rebecca, who has always made her living with her hands, either gardening or massaging. "Cleaning your house is like pruning a tree. The house and the tree are both alive. You take care of the debris first, then stand back to look at the true form—and that clarity, that original vision is what happens in the mind."

Stevie Smith, the British poet, commented that she dreamt up some of her best poems while "Hoovering." I have also opted for the vacuuming chores in my own household because the *rush* and *woosh* of the Kirby, and its solid paths on the thick carpet tell me where I've been, where I am, and exactly where I want to go.

All of us claim territory. Traditionally the masculine way is to mark territory by scent, by song, by a boast, a show of power, a pile of weapons: "This is mine, do not enter or you'll reckon with me!" The feminine claiming is perhaps a fierce physical possessing of the space by adorning home with spells, magic, or brightly waving scarves in trees, as do the aborigines, who put powerful altars near their hearths both for worship and to summon protective guardian spirits.

Once several years ago, upon hearing that our rental home was to be scrutinized by potential buyers, my two housemates and I broke all real estate rules by staying home and doing our Saturday morning chores. While the house buyers perused, I maneuvered the noisiest vacuum this side of Seattle; one housemate ran the dishwasher and slung wet laundry every-where, like so many volunteer scarecrow troops; my other housemate followed the harried home buyers from room to room wielding a defending dust mop. She actually sprayed the real estate agent with her lemon Pledge.

Cleaning has long been women's work. For years women have borne the archetype of body, darkness, the erotic, the un-clean, the Earth. This association has often imprisoned women in the home and thrust men into the world. Thus, leaving the home is traditionally associated with the heroic explorer, the powerful "man of the world," while housework is seen as triv-ial, timid, uninspired, menial labor left to servants. But we are all in service to our homes, as well as our homeland of Earth.

For years environmentalists have been educating us to rec-ognize that the whole wide world *is* our home; we cannot leave the world, or transcend it, or truly throw anything away. We must learn to be here. If women claim the world the way they already have their homes and if men claim their homes as fer-vently as they have the world, what might we create?

But instead of men and women creating their own homes, more and more people are leaving the home chores and ritual cleanings to hired hands. Are there some deep losses we all might incur from *not* cleaning up after ourselves? I suspect that doing our own chores is everyone's calling, no matter what our other important jobs. There is some sacredness in this daily, thoughtful, and very grounding housework that we cannot afford to lose if we are to be whole, integrated.

"Just getting down on my hands and knees and scouring the bathroom is like cleaning my soul," says a male friend. He adds with a laugh, "It shines—not necessarily my soul—but that white porcelain. And I feel new, like I've forgiven myself something."

Another of my men friends tells of his mother's death. When she, a meticulous cleaner, died, he stayed on alone in her house for three days and put everything right and tidy. "I felt very close to my mother then," he says. "After all, she had taught me how to clean."

Chores are a child's first work, though they are often presented in the form of play. Girls play house, and boys spend hours running toy trucks over miniature mud mountains. Before we even teach children to speak, we instruct them in their separate chores, and so we shape the world, the future. Somewhere along the line, society quit expecting boys to clean up their rooms, insisting they order the outside world instead. If I were a man, I would feel this as a loss, a wisdom and honor denied me and my home.

Among my friends, no matter what their living situation, cleaning is a crucial issue. Perhaps it is simply a symbol of how we treat what we love. Some people clean like Lady Macbeth—"Out, damned spot!" Others clean haphazardly, or methodically, earnestly or devotedly. One of my former housemates, Lynettie Sue, cleans as a way of understanding and organizing her life. From room to room she goes, sighing with satisfaction, as under her broom and dust rag and window-washing squeegee the world must give way to her scrutiny, her vision of a higher order suggested by perfectly folded sheets and a piano that looks spit shined. She is particularly imperious in the bathroom, being a microbiologist and knowing well that those telltale bits of black mold on the shower ceiling are unhealthy organisms. I teasingly beg her, "Don't take me to Comet-witz," when she suggests my upstairs bathroom looks like a biologist's field trip, "*not* cleaning concentration camp!" But I have found, under her diligence, a luxury that nothing except lounging in a hot, sparkling clean bathtub can give me.

Cleaning can be an art. I've often spent a Saturday morning dancing on the freeway of love right in the middle of my living room with Aretha and a vacuum. I admit to practicing arcane rites of exorcism as deep as psychoanalysis by simply cutting up ex-lovers' clothes to use as rags for those deep-down, won't-go-away cleaning jobs like stains on a rug, on a heart. Once cleaning came to my rescue when I received the final galley proofs for my novel in the mail with the dire red rubber stamp RETURN: 36-HOUR PROOF." What did I do with only three days to read and correct my entire book? I spent the first day and a half in a frenzy of old-fashioned, whirlwind spring cleaning that shook the spiders from the rafters and my soul. The book was a breeze after my walk-in winter closet.

When we clean up after ourselves, whether it's a spilled jar, a broken chair, a disorganized study, or a death, we can see and reflect upon our own life and perhaps envision a new way that won't be so broken, so violent, so unconscious. By cleaning up our own homes we take responsibility for ourselves and for preserving what we love. But if our attitude is "my kingdom is not of this world," then there is a disturbing possibility that we'll finally do away with the world rather than clean it or ourselves. The feminine attitude of getting down on our hands and knees to scour—and at the most primitive level look at what needs cleaning—deserves our attention. For in this gesture of bended knees is some humility, some meditation, some time to recognize the first foundation of our homes.

It was a simple washing machine and dryer that got me to

my knees that day my friend died—in horror, in mourning, in surrender not to death but to survival. It was a homing instinct that grounded me and made me want to stay on. To this day I have a ritual of running the washer and dryer while I am in my study at work. There is no more comforting sound to me than the spinning of that washer or dryer. It is the whole world spinning in there, cleansing itself and me.

As long as the washer and dryer spin, I tell myself, I am safe and those I love may choose to keep living alongside me. For there is laundry to be done and so many chores—chores of the living. There is so much to be remembered under the dust of our old contempt for cleaning up after ourselves, picking up our own socks. There is much to be swept away and shined bright and scrubbed down to its deepest, most illuminating level. Think of all the chores we have yet to do, quietly and on our knees—because home is holy.

HEARTBREAK HOTEL

OVER THE YEARS, IN RHYTHM TO THE EBB AND FLOW OF my romances, I've found myself checking in and out of a shelter I've come to call Heartbreak Hotel. Sometimes I go there in my mind, sometimes Heartbreak Hotel shares my actual street address; what is the same is what goes on here: a rest, a rite of passage, a healing, and finally a way of loving the world more truly because exiled from it.

In certain tribes when the heart suffers some death or loss, the women seclude themselves in the spiritual commune of the moon lodges while the men launch off into a long journey, perhaps a hunt or a vision quest. But in our peculiarly impatient and restless American way of intimacy, love on the lam, there is little time to practice this ritual of grief. Mourning is embarrassing, it is certainly antisocial, and sometimes it just seems downright rude.

And yet in Heartbreak Hotel I've discovered the welcome mat is always out for the weary, huddled masses of modern lovers who must seek shelter like so many homeless hearts. If in the old days there was the Foreign Legion for wounded-in-action soldiers and endless Edith Wharton ocean crossings for heroines with heart murmurs, today we need nearby getaways. That's why Heartbreak Hotels are never hard to find. They are just off the side streets of the great thoroughfares of romantic commerce. In fact, I've noticed them nowadays popping up like prefabs on the erotic market, even more insistently than the condo of the couple.

Heartbreak Hotels are quite distinct pieces of property, depending upon the dominant sexual character of the heart-broken or the relationship itself. The hotels are no longer seg-regated, for a woman might well need to check herself in at an unself-consciously seedy masculine Heartbreak Hotel at least for a belt of bourbon and milk; just as a man might be com-forted to be ensconced in the cozy breakfast nook of the femi-nine Heartbreak Hotel where a mammy who is also a wet nurse serves hot chocolate spiked with peppermint schnapps.

In the masculine Heartbreak Hotel the tenants never shave faces or legs; in the feminine Heartbreak Hotel, the lodgers eat popcorn and Snickers bars for supper. There is never sex; even flirtations make us flinch. In the feminine Heartbreak Hotel there are junk food deliveries made by stunning, but discreet and sympathetic, delivery people, all hours, all ears. One can order compassion with extra catsup or try a little tenderness with tartar sauce. But the delivery people, like the fast food they serve, have a schedule. They don't linger like any kind of real nourishment.

These delicious delivery people never go near the masculine Heartbreak Hotel. That's because in the masculine Heartbreak Hotel one doesn't eat, one drinks. There in the single resi-dences of this transient hotel, the heartbroken don't have stomachs. They have guts. This masculine Heartbreak Hotel looks out on the wrong side of town. A railroad or subway track shudders nearby; neon glares, unblinking. Beneath a naked bulb is a slim, steel bed, a tacky bedstand where Gideon's Bible has been hocked for Wild Turkey, Camel unfiltereds, a deck of cards, a pair of fingernail clippers. Clip, clip, drip, drip of the broken sink. One reads only the graffiti scrawled on the wall. Perhaps there is a *Playboy* or *Cosmopolitan* rolled up like a blunt weapon, repeatedly rapped against the thigh in rhythm to some hangover hum in the head. Occasionally there is the sound of the magazine striking a glancing blow to the wall. This is *not* a call for help, nor is it a statement. It is a reflex of the heart in solitary confinement—or perhaps on death row—awaiting not a pardon but the final zap, the poison, the noose. *Let it come,* says the single resident in this masculine Heartbreak Hotel, *I dare you to take me any further down than I can take myself.*

If the masculine Heartbreak Hotel is an inner battleground, the feminine Heartbreak Hotel is like a camp pitched near enough to see the smoke and hear the wails of the dying, the deserted, the damned. As in all camps, there is a coziness even in this most primitive of conditions, the death of the heart. Of course, there is a front porch with rockers stretching the length. There is the night music of crickets or waves of mountain wind—anything that sighs in sync with us. Rooms are comfy, familiar, often rearranged to fit moods, whims, or whirlwind, heartfelt tidy attacks. Favorite foods are baked potatoes, banana cream pie, pasta with gluttonous amounts of pesto and glorious garlic. Oreos are stashed in convenient crevices, as are sweet Sherman's cigarettes, sherry, and delicate, finger-sized Almond Joys. There is a small refrigerator in the large bathroom with a garret ceiling. It offers driest Chablis, champagne splits, and Diet Pepsi. There is a telephone, a bookshelf with Victorian novels—*Wuthering Heights* a favorite wallow—and a twenty-pound box of Mr. Bubble. Down the hall waft strains of Patsy Cline's "I Fall to Pieces" or Joni Mitchell's "Oh, I could drink a case of you, darling, and I would still be on my feet. . . ." Evenings in the feminine Heartbreak Hotel bring readings of old love letters, followed by well-meaning but sparsely attended workshops called "Intimacy in the 90s" or "Forgiveness 1A." Most lodgers wander off down memory lane, or onto the wide embrace of the front porch, up to the madwoman's attic, or into the softly lit, free massage and dream therapy rooms.

For all its luxurious mournfulness, the feminine Heartbreak Hotel is as difficult a stay as its masculine counterpart. To be so bereft while coddled by the familiar litter of one's love; to be alone yet surrounded by soulmates; to be in the dark during broad daylight—this is as dangerous a descent as the more daredevil masculine grief, the fighter jock who plays chicken with the Earth. For in the feminine Heartbreak Hotel, we are just as lost, no matter the trail we might leave of brightly colored M&M's or tea cozies.

It is in this willing wallow that the masculine and feminine Heartbreak Hotels meet. Yet there is a final, telling difference: length of stay. In the masculine Heartbreak Hotel, there are weekend, even hourly rates. As my friend Gregory says flatly, "No guy would ever max out his MasterCard at Heartbreak Hotel." But in the feminine Heartbreak Hotel, lodgers sometimes linger for life. This contrast is also one of the only drawbacks to Heartbreak Hotel. Masculine mourners tend to grieve on the run or in singles' bars, sometimes carrying their unburdened sorrow right into the next relationship. This leads to cynicism; a fist can clench and unclench quickly—not so the heart. Then there are the feminine lodgers who survive on maintenance sorrow, dolefully expecting lovers to follow rules made for delivery people. It would be sadder still if only men checked into the masculine Heartbreak Hotel and women into the feminine. This exclusivity only encourages the segregation and solipsism that sends us to Heartbreak Hotel in the first place.

The feminine Heartbreak Hotel can borrow from the masculine their larger-than-life battle that becomes a true rite of passage; from this our hearts learn courage and the resilience of a working muscle. The masculine Heartbreak Hotel can learn from the feminine to abide with one's own pain and take a rest from the front, from the warrior way, so that the heart might again embrace without fear, without expecting an enemy.

Whether we check into the masculine or feminine Heartbreak Hotel, whether we rent by the hour, the day, the year, and whether we even visit in the middle of current love affairs like a kind of halfway house, our Heartbreak Hotel awaits us. It will always wait to open and welcome us, just like another heart.

BATHING WITH
MADAME BOVARY

For L.B.

"IN DARK ALASKA WINTERS," A FISHERMAN FRIEND TOLD me, "if a man wants a woman's company, his cabin better have running water."

"Why?" I teased. "Don't you think women can rough it like men?"

"Sure they can." He grinned. "But women want hot baths in between. If you want to keep a woman in winter, water's the way."

I wondered at what my friend said—do baths belong more to the feminine than to the masculine? On an impromptu survey of my female friends, thirteen out of fifteen preferred baths to showers; of the same number of men asked, fourteen out of fifteen chose brisk showers over what one uncomfortable man called "stewing in my own juices."

As I write this now, I am in the tub. My skin is wonderfully wrinkled like stewed prunes, and the juices that steep my body are luxurious lavender, eucalyptus, and melissa balm. I imagine I'm in my own Caribbean cove with all I need surrounding me: glacial Bourassa bottled water to drink, Mozart on the headphones, a candle glowing inside delicate wax colored like stained-glass windows. Across the blue tub balances a pine board on which I have my writing pad, books, and loofah sponges. My feet now long for loofah and the rich cocoa butter massage that will soon coat and perfume these scoured feet as if I've just stepped from a vat of warm chocolate.

Every so often while writing, I sink beneath the tub desk and rest against my bath pillow shaped like a soft seashell to cushion my shoulders and sore neck. The triangle of trapezius muscles are a writer's bane; they seem always in spasm. But watery heat tenderly eases those knots and lets the muscles melt until they float the heavy head like so much seaweed flotsam adrift on a warm sea.

It is not the womb I'm after here; it is Neptunian nepenthe. I want to forget myself, loose the tense bonds and laws of gravity. The world flows and pulses with the feminine pull of Moon and ocean. Perhaps if our planet were a desert, our species might clean our skin with white sand. But as much as we Earth dwellers forget it, as single-minded as we were to name our entire planet for the only element we humans live upon—by rights this world should be named Sea, and maybe the whales call it that in their long, low lullabies—this planet orbiting the Sun looks so blue from outer space because seven-tenths of it belongs to water.

Why not then worship in the bath?

"What do you *do* in there for all that time?" an old boyfriend once asked me. There was a hint of fear in his voice, and fascination. "It's erotic, right?"

"What would you do if someone assigned you to take a bath for two hours?" I teased.

"Well. . . ." He brightened. "Maybe I'd make love to myself—that's the polite way of saying it."

"Then what?"

"I'd wash and scrub. . . ." He fell silent.

"Would you massage with expensive oils? Would you read Victorian novels or chat on the portable phone? Would you meditate or burn candles all round so that you floated in warmth and light like those bioluminescent creatures at the very bottom of the ocean who give off their own bright phosphorus as a by-product?"

"Stop!" he cried, both alarmed and lulled. "It's siren stuff. Your baths might as well be shipwreck for a man. We drown in mermaids' arms."

So I asked him into the bath. He chose sandalwood soap and almond milk bubbles. As we lay in the tub together, I washed his feet, then rubbed his back with strong sponges. Tenderly we washed each other's hair with chamomile shampoo and lemongrass conditioner. As we sipped sparkling cider from plastic wineglasses, he lay back and sighed, eyes closed. I had never seen him more relaxed or vulnerable. That bath was the only time he ever told me he was in love with me. Shortly afterward we broke up.

"It was that bath," he said, to explain why he was going back to his ex-wife. "We should have waited until we knew one another better before we did . . . *that*."

We'd been lovers half a year before this bath. But he was right. We weren't ready. It was more intimate than lovemaking.

It is ironic that in our twentieth-century love, nineteenth-century eroticism seems improper at best—at worst a direct threat. Flaubert knew about deep intimacies of the bath. In *Madame Bovary* Emma is pursued by an adoring Rodolphe, who declares, "Oh, I think of you constantly. . . . One cannot fight fate! Or resist when the angels sing!" The effect of Rodolphe's passionate words upon Madame is telling. "Emma had never been told such things before and her pride stretched out luxuriously in the warmth of his words, as though she were relaxing in a hot bath."

To the nineteenth-century reader, the sinking of Madame Bovary into bath instead of bed was synonymous with intimacy. Still today, European men seem to take more baths than their American counterparts. An editor friend often came across her Italian boyfriend sunk deep in his elaborate, claw-footed tub, mineral salts instead of bubbles. Sometimes he did business in the bath with Dictaphone and calculator. Another friend lived many years with a Frenchman whose passion was to disappear into the bath, turn off the lights, and listen to the Grateful Dead at full volume. A Cuban man I know takes afternoon baths like daily siestas.

I suspect one reason why most American men prefer showers is that they accept the Puritan equation between water and body. Showers are for baptism, cleaning, and cooling down unruly, too passionate flesh. One cleans one's body, lingering as little as possible on the sensual temptations of skin, curve, and private places. In contrast, when my stepgrandmother Vergie used to bathe us grandchildren in her tin washtub, she'd take a soft flannel cloth, suds it into a lather of Ivory, and proceed to "put y'all back together." Ever since she heard somewhere that the word *re-member* means to put back together a dismembered body, she saw her baths as a way of helping her grandchildren remember their bodies.

We learned the facts of life as we learned the lay of the land. Vergie taught us to take care of our bodies as she did her land. "Nothing sorrier than an old used-up person or field."

"Another thing," Vergie always finished her baths with a welcome cold rinse like a garden hose-down in midsummer. "No one owns your body but you. Just like nobody really owns the land."

If no one owns my body but me, who better to nurture and care for it than myself? If my body is my true home, why would I ever forsake or ravage it? Vergie is still very much alive, my only surviving grandparent. I believe her survival into active old age has much to do with tending her bountiful garden and taking good care of her own and others' bodies.

Bathing our children and grandchildren is a mothering gift; bathing lovers is a sacrament of sensual love. But I believe the best that baths can give us is the simple yet rare act of self-knowledge. *Know thyself*—this includes knowing bodies. Bathing calls forth a self-scrutiny. Certainly an hour afloat with one's own imperfect thighs, belly, and derriere, a bath familiar with one's own cellulite and flaccid fault lines, is an exercise in self-acceptance. It is hard to transcend the body in a hot bath. One sinks into one's own physical and metaphysical depths. Who knows what lurks down there? Who knows what we might plumb about ourselves? Will our compassion for what we discover about ourselves be equaled by our tendency toward self-contempt?

I keep two pictures in my bathroom: One is a painting of a naked woman swimming with dolphins; the other is a 1972 framed silver print by the famous *Life* photojournalist W. Eugene Smith. Called "Tomoko in Her Bath," the darkly lit black-and-white photo shows a young Japanese girl, victim of mercury poisoning from a nearby chemical factory, which caused birth defects in many of her village's children. Tomoko's truncated, shriveled body, her twisted hands like flippers useless and afloat beside her body are almost unbearable to look at for long. What makes staring at the photograph possible is the rapt, unflinching compassion of the woman who floats Tomoko in her wide arms, all the while gazing gently down upon the child in all her deformity. This woman's arms and eyes take in everything—from misshapen hands to withered legs to a head thrown back in numb, physical despair.

In my mind, this is an image of the divine Mother bathing her broken child. This Mother does not judge human deformity or condemn it to eternal punishment. This Mother's mercy is a clear-eyed witness to what cripples us. I have gazed deeply at this photo while lying in my own bath, whenever the deforming demons of my inner critic weigh heavily on me, body and soul. I have apprenticed myself to learning this kind of feminine compassion, which especially embraces what is most hideous and dark about me. This is true baptism to me. If God the Father's forgiveness of this world comes at the cost of sacrificing His Son, it is God the Mother who takes that body down from the cross and bathes its broken bones and fatal wounds.

The photographer of "Tomoko in Her Bath" was critically wounded as a war correspondent during the 1945 invasion of Okinawa. During his painful convalescence, he endured thirty-two operations. He well understood physical suffering and compassion. His heart-stirring photo essay "Minamata" (1975) exposed the chemical company's mercury poisoning of Japanese children to a horrified world. For his revelations, Smith was harassed, driven out of the village, and severely beaten. Many people believe that he never recovered from these beatings and that they led directly to his death in 1978. It is a sad irony that the compassion of a clear-eyed witness can be so dangerous.

Compassion for one's self and others is not a blissful denial nor is it an easy embrace of darkness. Seeing one's self clearly and witnessing others in all their wide range of being is often harrowing. And that is why in my bathroom there is that double vision to help me in my bath—the playfulness of the dolphins as well as the dive into my own darkness.

Perhaps this descent is what made one of the men in my survey uncomfortable; perhaps this is the "stewing" in one's own self that he so feared. Even Madame Bovary had to reckon with it and, so, herself. As Rodolphe, "certain of her love," retreated, he "began to be careless." Emma grieved: "Gone were those tender words that had moved her to tears, those tempestuous embraces that had sent her frantic, the grand passion into which she had plunged seemed to be dwindling around her like a river sinking into its bed; she saw the slime at the bottom." The water imagery is apt. While water cleanses, it can also be troubled, polluted, full of "slime." Madame Bovary has bathed in Rodolphe's love; she will also sink into it and ultimately not survive her descent.

These days while bathing I like to imagine a modern ending for *Madame Bovary*. Instead of killing herself for love lost, she decides to take to her bath. There she spends days comforting herself with Damask Rose and Devon Violet bath seeds. Adrift in the steaming flower fragrance, Madame Bovary opens her eyes and sees her own body so recently abandoned, so longing for her lost lover's touch. She takes a sponge, sudsed with sandalwood, and strokes her long arms, her delicate legs, her floating breasts. Emma sighs and slips deeper into the bath, luminous with bubbles. She notices that her own skin gleams, too.

Only now can she look deeper into the slime also growing at the bottom of her own life—the financial ruin, the emotional debts her passions have run up as high as her fevers. She is bankrupt, body and soul. Should she simply sigh and drown herself in this bath? Should she really gulp arsenic stolen from her local chemist? Softly Emma hears a deep and familiar feminine voice, as if the water herself were speaking, soothing, cleansing. Emma closes her eyes and imagines there are mothering arms rocking her, a dark and compassionate face gazing down upon her as she weeps into the warm water. Can she, like her lovers, truly abandon this broken body? Slowly Emma eases herself from the bath as if she is newborn, as if she has at last remembered herself.

PART II

Nature and Other Mothers

OTHER TEACHERS THAN TERROR—FROM DINOSAURS TO DOLPHINS

WHEN I WAS A CHILD, MY IMAGINARY FRIENDS WERE dinosaurs. My favorite was Brontosaurus, whom I often found foraging in the basement near our fallout shelter for the fierce survivor weeds growing up through cracks in the foundation cement.

Those days I, too, was a little survivor looking for openings in my parents' Southern fundamentalism, facing the terror of our Virginia hamlet's ground-zero neighbor, Washington, DC, and enduring our school's frequent civil defense drills.

Every time we ducked and covered—our teacher told us Russia had all its missiles aimed right at our hearts in the nation's capital, and I imagined when the bombs hit all our heads would explode in geysers of brilliant blood—I would call in my dinosaur troops. R. Tyranno would grab a bomb with those steel claws and hold it high until he could defuse it with his amazingly agile hands; Brontosaurus bent over me, a gentle bodyguard against shattering glass and flying desks or other children propelled midair like small, helpless human rockets;

Ichthyosaur (Iki, I called her) would swim in the air alongside me, waiting for the still moment when right there in the hurricane eye of the end-of-the-world, she'd offer me her dorsal fin and speed off to safety. I'd grab my brother and sisters, and we'd all hang on for dear life as Iki leaped and dived and carried us back to the sea. Then we'd all leave this dangerous land that was on fire and go back into the ocean, where we were all still little enough to remember how to breathe underwater.

That was my own civil defense plan. And, when I compared it with what our teacher told us about emergency evacuation by bus and military personnel, or my mother's fervent explanations of the Biblical Rapture, when God would lift cars and trucks and churches up into the air for eternity, my plan seemed a lot more practical.

Over the years I kept my civil defense strategies to myself, just as I hid my dinosaurs. Mostly they lived in our basement, R. Tyranno's great tail wrapped around the Ping-Pong table, and Iki out in the irrigation ditches running near our house. Brontosaurus holed up in the fallout shelter, but she was so big she filled the whole room with its shelves of canned food, distilled water, candles, the Bible, and a Monopoly game.

When I was in fifth grade, the world ended again for my dinosaurs. One day the teacher abruptly announced that we were all to go straight home—no duck-and-cover drill, just hide and hope the Russian missiles aiming at us from Cuba didn't seek. It was the late autumn of 1962, the week that would culminate in Black Saturday, when the world came the closest to nuclear war since Hiroshima. Schools dismissed, people set to stock-piling food and supplies, their fallout shelters fully operational. This was no test, the teacher said; this was real. "Go home, children," she'd said more softly than we ever imagined her voice could be.

We all stampeded home like animals fleeing before a forest fire—eyes wide and white. "What's happening? What's happening?" R. Tyranno and Bronto were nowhere to be found. Iki guided us home.

Mother met me at the door and sent all of us kids straight down to the fallout shelter. There was no chance to follow Iki back to the sea. Instead, we were buried alive in our basement shelter. We hid, candles flickering as we listened to the transistor radio. President Kennedy's Yankee voice crackled and warned the Russians to withdraw their missiles from Cuba or face retaliation. I'd seen pictures of Cuba and Castro, a man who looked like a Neanderthal in a drab baseball cap smoking a cigar. I could believe that someone with a face like that might start a war.

Strangely calm, we all sat in the semidarkness of our shelter, wondering if our father, with his top-security clearance, would stay in DC or come home to us. As I gazed around at my siblings, their faces ancient and familiar in the candle firelight like a tribe long before civilization, I felt so sad. They were too little to die. But I was not afraid, not until the moment I glanced up and at last saw my beautiful Brontosaurus. Curled around her great self, she was so terrified that basement weeds still hung from her mouth, uneaten.

Terror takes away hunger, I realized; there is a different kind of hunger, and that has to do with simply wanting, more than anything else in the world, to live. I recognized this other hunger in my Bronto's eyes—the biggest eyes I'd ever seen, dark and deep and afraid to die.

"There's . . . ," I began, not knowing I spoke aloud, "there's not enough room. . . ."

"No, no, we have plenty of air," my mother answered me, already somewhat panicky from her own claustrophobia.

But I wasn't speaking to her; I was talking to Bronto, who, coiled like a stricken leviathan, gazed at me with pity and fear and understanding. My sisters and brother all seemed as giddy and grim as my mother. They played Monopoly and ate three Whitman Samplers my mother had stashed for just such an emergency.

So there, during the Cuban missile crisis, I watched my sisters put hotels on Park Place and ruin my little brother's meager Oriental properties. I watched my mother fall into a drowsy trance, from either the chocolate or lack of oxygen. We would not last, I knew. I never had to ask my beloved Brontosaurus. Without a cry, without a protest, with only a tender gaze in her great eye, she let herself out of that fallout shelter and out of my world. She joined R. Tyranno and Iki and went to where everything extinct goes—maybe where we would go.

My only imaginary friend that did not die out during the Cuban missile crisis was Iki, the prehistoric dolphin. Even inside the concrete tank of our fallout shelter, I sensed that my Ichthyosaurus still swam freely in oceans that nuclear fire could not burn. All the land creatures might die in an atomic flash, but the wide, blue oceans would survive. And from these vast saltwater wombs another species would live on. That's where everyone I loved would be—under the sea.

My family stayed in that fallout shelter until late that night, when my father found us. For the rest of that week, we spent so much time in our shelter that we depleted our supplies; by Black Saturday we were cranky, hungry, sick of sweets, and ready to kill one another. I still have a pointed scar on my left wrist from my sister's thumbnail; she dug in astonishingly deep when I lucked out, didn't land on her row of low-class hotels, and instead went directly to jail.

The morning the Russians finally relented and we surprised ourselves by actually being happy to go to school, I walked through the woods, calling to my dinosaurs to come back. But they stayed gone so long that I at last realized they didn't *want* to come back and be here in the world with me. And for the first time I understood that there is a part of all of us that doesn't want to be here. Why else would we have decided to blow up our home and go extinct?

•   •   •

It's been over three decades since I lost my imaginary friends in that fallout shelter. In that time the unthinkable has happened: we've had no nuclear war. Instead, the Berlin Wall has collapsed and, with it, our old enemy, Russia. Recently the minute-to-midnight clock was set back, and many Russian and American nuclear arms are now aimed away from human targets and into the sea instead. I'm sure this doesn't comfort Iki and her generations of dolphins; but it is supposed to reassure our species and thus signal an end to the Cold War. But the political declaration of an end to the mutual destruction of two superpowers does not mean we have transcended terror. And those generations of us who were taught to duck and cover have yet to plumb the depths of what it means to have grown up expecting the world to end.

Our parents' generation was bred on Depression-era fears of loss and totalitarian tyrants who engage in world wars. But in WWI and WWII, there was always the anticipation of human survival. It is the prospect of a WWIII without survivors, including our planet, that every generation since Hiroshima has reckoned with, either consciously or unconsciously. And this terror of apocalypse is so wired into our collective psyche, our physical bodies, and our spiritual seekings that we must continually ask ourselves to face first our own darkness, our inner enemies, our species' death wish.

The original Greek meaning of the word *apokalypsis* is "revelation." And certainly we've all witnessed in some form the shocking flash of light from an atomic bomb—but have we yet been illumined by this brilliant light? While the prospect of nuclear war has forced us into some well-needed restraint, it has not taught us how to heal the terror we were nursed upon like mother's milk. Post–Cold War we have translated our nuclear terror into new end-of-the-world scenarios: environmental apocalypse, sexual and bacterial plagues, national and international terrorism.

Once an ex-Buddhist priest told me, "Your soul has learned about itself through the vehicle of crisis." I wondered if perhaps the priest was not only speaking about me, but about many post–Cold War people. We are desperately trying to deny, soothe, transcend, or understand the terror that has taken hold of our species. As we children of the Cold War enter a new century, can we as adults find some mature calm and clarity? Can we truly find other teachers than terror?

After over forty years of facing what I'd call my own family's "emergency personality," I've found that I'm not looking for antidotes to terror so much as alternative teachers. And I've found many. I've apprenticed myself to several physical, spiritual, and psychological practices to center and calm my ingrained patterns of terror. All these disciplines have deeply eased much of the anxiety of my duck-and-cover childhood.

But there are lessons I yet seek as I enter a new century and my own middle age. I would like to know how to find deep calm and mature clarity even in the midst of terrorizing events all around me. In my own search for illumination, I have reached out as an adult to the same fellow creature whom I hoped would save me as a child—the cetacean, or dolphin. Dolphins have convinced me that there are other teachers than terror. Dolphins spend three-quarters of their lives at play. I'm wondering if play might be a form of survival for *our* species, for play is all about discovering new skills that may help a species evolve.

Of all the animals, human and nonhuman, I've encountered, the dolphins, descendants of Ichthyosaurus, most embody a calm and happy spirit. For a decade now I've been studying and swimming with the same group of female bottlenose dolphins in the Florida Keys. Every summer I also go whale watching along the Pacific Coast—from California to the San Juan Islands near Victoria, B.C. Winters, I follow the humpback and spinner dolphins to Hawaii and the gray whales to Mexico breeding lagoons.

Now my dreams teem with cetaceans. One night I dreamed of a luminous white dolphin who beached herself purposefully to lie in my arms as I sat in the waves with her, midwifing four newborns. In my dream I saw what I later discovered with a shock of recognition in a textbook: dolphin and human fetuses are, eerily, anatomic mirror images of one another.

There have been many shocks of recognition in my lifelong apprenticeship to the dolphin mind. Some of them have happened underwater when I found myself eye-to-unblinking eye with a dolphin mother that allowed her calf to leap over my legs, his silken belly sliding against my skin. Other times I've recognized the deep intelligence in a dark dolphin eye as she studied me, her graceful, sloping head turned sideways as she scanned with her 360-degree overlapping vision. Most recently I recognized the feeling of pure rapture as I watched Bogie, Bacall, and Molly—three female dolphins being rehabilitated in the Sugarloaf Dolphin Sanctuary in Sugarloaf Key, Florida—shoot straight out of the water in perfect sync, somersault together, and then splash down into the large saltwater lagoon, leaving several of us on the dock sopping wet. They were not performing a show for us; they were playing together, perhaps anticipating their release into open waters near their original pods.

Molly swam over to me and turned her head in scrutiny. As she eyed me, I remembered a marine biologist friend telling me that a dolphin's eyesight is as good above the surface as underwater and that dolphins rely on eye contact as a major form of social interaction. There was curiosity and kindness in Molly's deep gaze; I felt myself fully met and somehow known. As she bobbed there in the warm water, holding my gaze, I realized how seldom I really look at other humans with such calm and openness. And Molly had no reason to engage me with such trust. For twenty-five years Molly was a show dolphin in small carnivals. She was carted around in the back of a station wagon from town to town; her body is covered with scars from such haphazard travel. Yet Molly gazed at me with such trust and affection that I had to look down, humbled by her gaze. Then, in one subtle motion, Molly slipped her slender, long snout beneath my forearm. Suddenly I felt rapid-fire bursts of her sonar against my skin. My arm vibrated with Molly's sonar song and I felt again the thrill of interspecies physical contact.

It reminded me of the time when a friend and I were swimming with another group of dolphins. Underwater I gazed through my snorkel mask and watched in astonishment as two 600-pound dolphins, Dreamer and Sara, flanked my friend. With their fins, the two dolphins actually embraced her, belly-to-belly, and the trio slowly corkscrewed through the water in a kind of human-dolphin dance. I had never before seen dolphins take another human in their fins and I probably never will again.

No wonder, I thought then, that as a child I chose a dolphin ancestor, Ichthyosaurus, to be my guide and carry me through what seemed to be the End of the World. No wonder that in the midst of a Cold War aimed at destroying not only all human and animal life but also the entire planet, I reached out to a species which has survived for millions of years. No wonder all my dinosaurs went extinct except Iki. There was something in these dolphins that held dearly to life and even to humans, their mammal kin. Was this why the ancient Greeks honored dolphins and believed they carried the souls of the dead safely through this final passage to the underworld?

The Greek root word for dolphin (classified as *Delphimus delphis*) is *delphys* which means "womb." The famous Delphic Oracle was originally a revered high priestess with the title Pythia, Dragon Priestess of the Earth. She was named after the divine python snake who was also sometimes portrayed as a

Delphyne or womb-monster. For over two thousand years, this Pythia priestess revealed her oracular wisdom to the ancient Greek world from Delphi, which was called the Navel of the Earth. It was this powerful feminine python whom Apollo was said to have slain to establish his own oracular shrine. Apollo assumed the title Delphinics or "dolphin god," and began a festival, Delphinia, to celebrate his victory.

The sun god's conquest of the womb-monster signalled the mythic and cultural assumption that Apollo the god—certainly not any goddess—was now in control of the world's womb. Apollo was also worshipped in his dolphin body as the death god who carried Greek souls back to their womb-tomb and the Land of the Dead. Apollo was called upon and praised in the cycles of Greek tragedies which hoped to arouse "pity and terror" as a sign of artistic success.

But few characters survived in these tragedies. This is the inheritance that Western Greek-based civilization has given me. But in my childhood choice of imaginary friends such as Ichthyosaurus—who did not go extinct like the dinosaurs—perhaps I was remembering a more ancient, feminine story of the sea-womb or *delphys*-dolphin which can never be slain by a sun god or a fire-bomb. Tragedy and a species such as the dinosaur, whose story was extinction, could not carry me safely through the underworld of my Cold War childhood; only the dolphins could carry me back to the womb, that living sea which gives birth to all.

In reclaiming a species which does not go extinct, I place myself in another ancient tradition which chooses comedy over tragedy, the simple glory of survival over the tragic end. And now that the sun god Apollo, with his nuclear wars, has failed in slaying our species, perhaps the ancient feminine mysteries and oracles will return. The Greek Oracle always taught, "Know Thyself." A question for the 21st century could be, "How to live now that we've decided not to destroy ourselves?"

That day as I sat on a warm Florida Keys dock, letting a dolphin lift my arm with her glossy snout, I realized that my decade of studying this other species had convinced me that: *there are other teachers than terror*—perhaps even play might be a form of survival. As if reading my mind, Molly suddenly dove straight down and leapt up before me, a *twoosh, twoosh* of air exhaled from that bright blowhole at its usual 100 m.p.h. velocity. Her great breath was so strong and vibrant, it washed over me like a warm wind.

Dolphins spend three-quarters of their entire lives in play. Is that what they're doing with those big brains and their hologrammatic intelligence? On the far side of the sanctuary's large lagoon, three other male dolphins—Luther, Buck, and Jake—echoed Molly's playful leaps. These dolphins had just arrived at the Sugarloaf Sanctuary after honorable discharge from the U.S. Navy. They, too, were being rehabilitated for release into the wild. These ex-military and ex-show dolphins were now catching live fish in preparation for their future foraging for food in the open oceans. As the dolphins raced around the lagoon, their vocalizations a symphony of clicks, clatters, rachets and whistles, I thought about the fact that both female and male dolphins are the same size, their gender also not marked by any difference in color.

I wondered what humans might be like if men and women were the same size, and if our families were focused on nurturing the young and on group communication survival skills? If we humans had the inner sonar power to stun any predator, would we be buried under our arsenals of nuclear weapons—which equal 250 tons of TNT for every man, woman, and child in the world? If human adults were the same size, would we be less suceptible to terror, and more involved in play? Would we raise our children with less violence and more imagination to envison a future in which we all survive?

When I ponder the history of human war, I can't help but

wonder, why are there no dolphin wars? Why do animals not slaughter entire other species or commit mass murder against their own kind? Dolphins have a unique way of dealing with aggression among themselves. If a young dolphin is too aggressive, his mother will forcibly butt him to teach him proper pod boundaries. If the aggression continues, the mother and perhaps an elder dolphin will evoke the most dreaded experience for any cetacean—they will, by holding the young dolphin underwater, suggest drowning.

When a dolphin calf is disciplined by being dunked underwater and held, this breathless reprimand is usually enough to deter aggression within the pod. But should that calf's aggressive behavior persist, and in rare cases it does, the dolphin pod will simply and absolutely shut out that individual dolphin. They will not respond to his sonar cries, his frequencies; though he may swim alongside them, they will no longer acknowledge his existence. The exiled dolphin will languish behind the pod, utterly dejected. He will either leave the pod and become a rare, lone dolphin, or he will stop feeding, though the fish be all around him. Finally, he will die of loneliness and abandonment. A dolphin's intense need for affection and a highly developed emotional life is the survival tool that has resulted from this very different evolution.

Humans, by contrast, have often promoted the most aggressive individuals and chosen an intelligence that favors strategic thinking, defense of the group, and goal-oriented communication. Our human brain size has evolved in response to the stimulus of stress and survival of the fittest. It is no coincidence that here on the brink of a new, more conscious evolution, we must consider that stress itself has become our most insidious health hazard. Stress—once our evolutionary trigger—is now our killer. It is a survival tool that needs to be retooled.

Dolphins are also very sensitive to stress; they often die of ulcers or, if they are severely depressed as is often the case in captivity, they will simply stop eating and consciously end their own lives. But along with their sensitivity to stress is a remarkable capacity for imaginative and social play.

I believe dolphins have a big head start on our species in exploring and developing their relationships and their inner worlds. If we humans weren't so busy with our hands, always making and manipulating nature, we might imagine what life would be like floating without gravity, communicating with our equally powerful peers, and turning inward. Scientists have tracked brain waves of cetaceans and found that they exist in a perpetual alpha or delta state, a meditative and highly creative state. Humans spend much of their time in beta brain waves, a more superficial and less deeply attentive mindset.

On another trip to the warm Florida waters, I was tooling around in the lush Everglade Keys when our small boat was greeted by two wild bottlenose dolphins.

"Hold on for dear life and we'll play with them!" called the naturalist ranger who was driving our boat, revving up the small motor to 40 m.p.h.

In a kind of slow-motion whiplash we shot forward, skimming along the backwaters with peregrine falcons and pelicans. Suddenly behind us in our roiling white wake were the two wild dolphins, swimming belly up, the better to see us. I leaned way back over the wild wake, my arms outstretched. The dolphins seemed to take this as a signal, an invitation. They disappeared momentarily, then shot straight up through our wake to fly inches beneath my hands. I gasped and laughed, screaming with pleasure. I knew my high-pitched calls were registering on their supersonic frequency and I started singing at the top of my voice.

"They *like* it," the ranger shouted.

Soon all five of us in the motorboat were singing and calling to the wild dolphins, encouraging their every leap and dive.

My face and hands were skimming the water now and one

of the wild dolphins cruised just beneath the wake, his eye fixed steadily on mine. In that dolphin's gaze was such benevolence that I had to smile, so thankful that long ago the child in me realized that not all my imaginary friends were extinct.

"Iki," I called softly to that wild dolphin flying alongside me. *I'll remember this wild dolphin, when I'm on my deathbed,* I found myself thinking suddenly. On the day that I go extinct, on the day I slip into the warm waters of my own final dive, my last breach and breath, I expect the dolphins will carry me over to the other side, just as now in life we carry on together.

Our boat finally slowed its pace and the dolphins leapt up once, then splashed us as if to take their playful leave. I watched that familiar arc and curve of fin in the turquoise ocean. The sun was setting and only the silhouettes of the dolphins showed against the vast pink horizon.

I shaded my eyes from the slant of the last, long rays of sun rippling across the water, still feeling the presence of the dolphins. Physicists theorize that by the simple act of observing something outside ourselves, we change that object. But I have felt more changed by the dolphins than perhaps they have by my scrutiny and embrace. Perhaps I am becoming less or more human. All I know is that just as I was a child of the Cold War, I am also profoundly imprinted by this other species' intelligence and kindness. In the South, they call this deep regard for the other witnessing.

When we witness one another, when we open ourselves to allow another species to observe, teach, and change us, there is much healing in the humility. And there is something else—companionship—as we learn the lessons of long life. I have not yet completely healed my duck-and-cover childhood. But I have found these other teachers than terror. In exchanging a calm, clear gaze with another species, we are reminded of a true alternative to fear: We are not here alone.

ANIMAL ALLIES

"My imaginary friend really lived once," the teen-age girl began, head bent, her fingers twisting her long red hair. She stood in the circle of other adolescents gathered in my Seattle Arts and Lectures storytelling class at the summer Seattle Academy. Here were kids from all over the city—every color and class, all strangers to one another. Over the next two weeks we would become a fierce tribe, telling our own and our tribe's story. Our first assignment was to introduce our imaginary friends from childhood. This shy fourteen-year-old girl, Sarah, had struck me on the first day because she always sat next to me, as if under my wing, and though her freckles and stylish clothes suggested she was a popular girl, her demeanor showed the detachment of someone deeply preoccupied. She never met my eye, nor did she join in the first few days of storytelling when the ten boys and four girls were regaling one another with futuristic characters called Shiva and Darshon, Masters of the Universe. So far the story lines we'd imagined were more Pac-Man than drama. After the first two days I counted a legion of characters killed off in intergalactic battle. The settings for all these stories portrayed the earth as an environmental wasteland, a ruined shell hardly shelter to anything animal or human. One of the girls called herself Nero the White Wolf and wandered the blackened tundra howling her powerful despair; another girl was a unicorn whose horn always told the truth. All the stories were full of plagues and nuclear wars—even though this is the generation that has witnessed the fall of the Berlin Wall, the end of the Cold War. Their imaginations have been shaped by a childhood story line that anticipates the end of this world.

After three days of stories set on an earth besieged by disease and barren of nature, I made a rule: No more characters or animals could die this first week. I asked if someone might imagine a living world, one that survives even our species.

It was on this third day of group storytelling that Sarah jumped into the circle and told her story:

"My imaginary friend is called Angel now because she's in heaven, but her real name was Katie," Sarah began. "She was my best friend from fourth to tenth grade. She had freckles like me and brown hair and more boyfriends—sometimes five at a time—because Katie said, 'I *like* to be confused!' She was a real sister, too, and we used to say we'd be friends for life. . . ." Sarah stopped, gave me a furtive glance and then gulped in a great breath of air like someone drowning, about to go down. Her eyes fixed inward, her voice dropped to a monotone. "Then one day last year, Katie and I were walking home from school and a red sports car came up behind us. Someone yelled, 'Hey, Katie!' She turned . . . and he blew her head off. A bullet grazed my skull, too, and I blacked out. When I woke up, Katie was gone, dead forever." Sarah stopped, stared down at her feet and murmured in that same terrible monotone, "Cops never found her murderer, case is closed."

All the kids shifted and took a deep breath, although Sarah herself was barely breathing at all. "Let's take some time to write," I told the kids and put on a cello concerto for them to listen to while they wrote. As they did their assignment, the kids glanced over surreptitiously at Sarah, who sat staring at her hands in her lap.

I did not know what to do with her story; she had offered it to a group of kids she had known but three days. It explained her self-imposed exile during lunch hours and while waiting for the bus. All I knew was that she'd brought this most important story of her life into the circle of storytellers and it could not be ignored as if *she* were a case to be closed. This story lived in her, would define and shape her young life. Because she had given it to us, we needed to witness and receive—and perhaps tell it back to her in the ancient tradition of tribal call and response.

"Listen," I told the group as the cello faded and they looked up from their work. "We're going to talk story the way they used to long ago when people sat around at night in circles just like this one. That was a time when we still listened to animals and trees and didn't think ourselves so alone in this world. Now we're going to carry out jungle justice and find Katie's killer. We'll call him before our tribe. All right? Who wants to begin the story?"

All the Shivas and Darshons and Masters of the Universe volunteered to be heroes on this quest. Nero the White Wolf asked to be a scout. Unicorn, with her truth-saying horn, was declared judge. Another character joined the hunt: Fish, whose translucent belly was a shining "soul mirror" that could reveal one's true nature to anyone who looked into it.

A fierce commander of this hunt was Rat, whose army of computerized comrades could read brain waves and call down lightning lasers as weapons. Rat began the questioning and performed the early detective work. Katie, speaking from beyond the earth, as Sarah put it, gave us other facts. We learned that two weeks before Katie's murder, one of her boyfriends was shot outside a restaurant by a man in the same red car—

another drive-by death. So Sarah had not only seen her best friend killed at her side, but she had also walked out into a parking lot to find Katie leaning over her boyfriend's body. For Sarah, it had been two murders by age thirteen.

With the help of our myriad computer-character legions we determined that the murderer was a man named Carlos, a drug lord who used local gangs to deal cocaine. At a party Carlos had misinterpreted Katie's videotaping her friends dancing as witnessing a big drug deal. For that, Rat said, "This dude decides Katie's got to go down. So yo, man, he offs her without a second thought."

Bad dude, indeed, this Carlos. And who was going to play Carlos now that all the tribe knew his crime? I took on the role, and as I told my story I felt my face hardening into a contempt that carried me far away from these young pursuers, deep into the Amazon jungle where Rat and his computer armies couldn't follow, where all their space-age equipment had to be shed until there was only hand-to-hand simple fate.

In the Amazon, the kids changed without effort, in an easy shape-shifting to their animal selves. Suddenly there were no more Masters of the Universe with intergalactic weapons— there was instead Jaguar and Snake, Fish and Pink Dolphin. There was powerful claw and all-knowing serpent, there was Fish who could grow big and small, and a dolphin whose sonar saw past the skin. We were now a tribe of animals, pawing, running, invisible in our jungle, eyes shining in the night, seeing Carlos as he canoed the mighty river, laughing because he did not know he had animals tracking him.

All through the story, I'd kept my eye on Sarah who played the role of her dead friend. The detachment I'd first seen in her was in fact the deadness Sarah carried, the violence that had hollowed her out inside, the friend who haunted her imagination. But now her face was alive, responding to each animal's report of tracking Carlos. She hung on the words, looking suddenly very young, like a small girl eagerly awaiting her turn to enter the circling jump rope.

"I'm getting away from you," I said, snarling as I'd imagined Carlos would. I paddled my canoe and gave a harsh laugh, "I'll escape, easy!"

"No!" Sarah shouted. "Let *me* tell it!"

"Tell it!" her tribe shouted.

"Well, Carlos only thinks he's escaping," Sarah smiled, waving her hands. "He's escaped from so many he's harmed before. But I call out 'FISH!' And Fish comes. He swims alongside the canoe and grows bigger, bigger until at last Carlos turns and sees this HUGE river monster swimming right alongside him and that man is afraid because suddenly Fish turns his belly up to Carlos's face. Fish forces him to look into that soul mirror. Carlos *sees* everyone he's ever killed and all the people who loved them and got left behind. And Carlos sees Katie and me and what he's done to us. He sees everything and he knows his soul is black. And he really doesn't want to die now because he knows then he'll stare into his soul mirror forever. But Fish makes him keep looking until Carlos starts screaming he's sorry, he's so sorry. Then . . . Fish *eats* him!"

The animals roared and cawed and congratulated Sarah for calling Fish to mirror a murderer's soul before taking jungle justice. Class had ended, but no one wanted to leave. We wanted to stay in our jungle, stay within our animals—and so we did. I asked them to close their eyes and call their animals to accompany them home. I told them that some South American tribes believe that when you are born, an animal is born with you. This animal protects and lives alongside you even if it's far away in an Amazon jungle. Because it came into the world the same time you did, it also dies with you to guide you back into the spirit world.

The kids decided to go home and make animal masks, returning the next day wearing the faces of their chosen animal.

When they came into class the next day it was as if we never left the Amazon. Someone dimmed the lights, there were drawings everywhere of jaguars and chimps and snakes. Elaborate masks had replaced the Masters of the Universe who began this tribal journey. We sat behind our masks in a circle with the lights low and there was an acute, alert energy running between us, as eyes met behind animal faces.

I realize that I, who grew up wild in the forest, who first memorized the earth with my hands, have every reason to feel this familiar animal resonance. But many of these teen-agers have barely been in the woods; in fact, many inner-city kids are *afraid* of nature. They would not willingly sign up for an Outward Bound program or backpacking trek; they don't think about recycling in a world they believe already ruined and in their imaginations abandoned for intergalactic nomad futures. These kids are not environmentalists who worry about saving nature. And yet, when imagining an Amazon forest too thick for weapons to penetrate, too primitive for their futuristic Pac-Man battles, they return instinctively to their animal selves. These are animals they have only seen in zoos or on television, yet there is a profound identification, an ease of inhabiting another species that portends great hope for our own species's survival. Not because nature is "out there" to be saved or sanctioned, but because nature is *in* them. The ancient, green world has never left us though we have long ago left the forest.

What happens when we call upon our inner landscape to connect with the living rainforests still left in the natural world? I believe our imagination can be as mutually nurturing as an umbilical cord between our bodies and the planet. As we told our Amazon stories over the next week of class, gathered in a circle of animal masks, we could feel the rainforest growing in that sterile classroom. Lights low, surrounded by serpents, the jaguar clan, the elephants, I'd as often hear growls, hisses, and howls as words. Between this little classroom and the vast Amazon rainforest stretched a fine thread of story that grew thicker each day, capable of carrying our jungle meditations.

When Elephant stood in the circle and said simply, "My kind are dying out," there was outrage from the other animals.

"We'll stop those poachers!" cried Rat and Chimp. "We'll call Jaguar clan to protect you." And they did.

This protection is of a kind that reaches the other side of the world. Children's imagination is a primal force, just as strong as lobbying efforts and boycotts and endangered species acts. When children claim another species as not only their imaginary friend, but also as the animal within them—their ally— doesn't that change the outer world?

This class believes it to be so. They may be young, but their memories and alliances with the animals are very old. By telling their own animal stories they are practicing ecology at its most profound and healing level. Story as ecology—it's so simple, something we've forgotten. In our environmental wars the emphasis has been on saving species, not *becoming* them. We've fallen into an environmental fundamentalism that calls down hellfire and brimstone on the evil polluters and self-righteously struts about protecting other species as if we are gods who can save their souls.

But the animals' souls are not in our hands. Only our own souls are within our ken. It is our own spiritual relationship to animals that must evolve. Any change begins with imagining ourselves in a new way. And who has preserved their imaginations as a natural resource most deeply? Not adults, who so often have strip-mined their dreams and imagination for material dross. Those who sit behind the wheel of a Jaguar have probably forgotten the wild, black cat that first ran with them as children. Imagination is relegated to nighttime dreams, which are then dismissed in favor of "the real world." But children, like some adults, know that the real world stretches farther than what we can see—that's why they shift easily between visions of our tribal past and our future worlds. The limits of the adult world are there for these teen-agers, but they still have a foot in the vast inner magic of childhood. It is this magical connection I called upon when I asked the kids to do the Dance of the Animals.

The day of the big dance I awoke with a sharp pain at my right eye. Seems my Siamese cat Ivan, who has always slept draped around my head, had stretched and his claw caught the corner of my eye. In the mirror I saw a two-inch scratch streaking from my eye like jungle make-up or a primitive face-painting. "The mark of the wildcat," the kids pronounced it when I walked into the dimly lit room to be met by a circle of familiar creatures. Never in ten years had my Siamese scratched my face. I took it as a sign that the dance began in his animal dream.

I put on my cobra mask and hissed a greeting to Chimp, Rat, Jaguar, and Unicorn. Keen eyes tracked me from behind colorful masks. I held up my rain stick which was also our talking stick and called the creatures one by one into the circle. "Sister Snake!" I called. "Begin the dance!"

Slowly, in rhythm to the deep, bell-like beat of my Northwest Native drum, each animal entered the circle and soon the dance sounded like this: Boom, step, twirl, and slither and stalk and snarl and chirp and caw, caw. Glide, glow, growl, and whistle and howl and shriek and trill and hiss, hiss. Each dance was distinct—from the undulating serpent on his belly, to the dainty high hoofing of Unicorn, from the syncopated stomps of Chimp on all-fours to Rat's covert jitterbug behind the stalking half-dark Jaguar. We danced, and the humid, lush jungle filled this room.

In that story line stretching between us and the Amazon, we connected with those animals and their spirits. And in return, we were complete—with animals as soul mirrors. We remembered who we were, by allowing the animals inside us to survive.

The dance is not over as long as we have our animal partners. When the kids left our last class, they still wore their masks fiercely. I was told that even on the bus they stayed deep in their animal character. I like to imagine those strong, young animals out there now in this wider jungle. I believe that Rat will survive the inner-city gangs; that Chimp will find his characteristic comedy even as his parents deal with divorce; I hope that Unicorn will always remember her mystical truth-telling horn. And as for Sarah who joined the Jaguar clan, elected as the first girl-leader over much mutinous boy-growling—Sarah knows the darkness she stalks and the nightmares that stalk her. She has animal eyes to see, to find even a murderer. Taking her catlike, graceful leave, she handed me a poem she'd written, "Now I can see in the dark," she wrote; and she signed herself, "Jaguar—future poet."

BELUGA BABY

A MAN BENDS OVER TO EMBRACE THE GLEAMING GRAY newborn beluga; his mouth presses against its tiny, unbreathing blowhole. The calf's small black eyes still move on each side of his domed head as he struggles for air. Gasping, the biologist breathes life into this small whale, cradling him in his arms as all around the zoo staff shout, "Breathe, breathe!" But the baby beluga is still, eyes fixed wide open. He never takes a breath; he dies in the man's arms.

These biologists at the Point Defiance Zoo in Tacoma, Washington, have to make a terrible decision: Should they allow the mother beluga to keep her dead calf as in the wild, or should the staff whisk the newborn away for a necropsy to determine the cause of death? Science at last wills out, and the staff removes the calf from the cold, bloody pool, leaving Mauyak, the mother beluga, to thrash about in confusion and pain.

Another staff member, Alan, stays with Mauyak for three hours after the birth. "She kept rolling over the scuba divers in a slow-motion embrace, trying to understand," he told me when I visited the zoo after the sorrowful birth. "This was, after all, Mauyak's first delivery," he explained. "And I don't know if she even realized her calf was dead before they took him away. There were two guys in the pool with two whales, Mauyak and the young female Shikku. Neither beluga had ever experienced birth, but we hoped Shikku would act as a midwife the way whales in the wild do for each other. The midwife whale will lift the newborn to the surface for its first breath. But as it turns out, Shikku didn't have to swim the calf to the surface, because after a very difficult labor—Mauyak corkscrewing and twisting in the small pool for hours—the little calf struggled out, tail flukes first, and floated himself to the surface.

"Everyone started cheering and clapping, because they believed the baby took a breath. But the calf just floated up there too quietly, then started sinking. Shikku and Mauyak lifted the little calf back up to the surface, and I yelled to another researcher to grab the calf and pull him up on the float to see if he was breathing. That's when we realized the calf had never taken his first breath. Our artificial respiration was hopeless because, as we later found out from the necropsy, his blowhole valve was disengaged, broken somehow . . . perhaps in all the labor. But we don't really know why. Belugas—especially their birthing—are such a mystery. Fifty percent of first-borns die, even in the wild."

I was walking with Alan and a photographer friend down to the zoo's Rocky Shores exhibit, home to three beluga whales: Mauyak, Shikku, and a male named Inuk. We walked slowly as Alan told his story. Outside the entrance to the big chilly pool with its glass underwater wall—through which zoo-goers can be eye-to-eye with a great beluga—Alan hesitated. "I haven't been back here since the birth, I mean the death," he said softly, his brown eyes pensive. "Mauyak may still be angry with me—with all of us."

"Did Mauyak ever get a chance to say good-bye to her calf?" I asked.

Alan lowered his voice. "No," he said.

As we approached the pool, Shikku and Inuk greeted Alan, whom they've known for over four years, with the chirps and whistles that earn this white whale the name "sea canary." But Mauyak swam immediately away to the back pool, a red rubber buoy balanced on her huge, pale forehead. "A whale will carry her dead newborn like that until it disintegrates," Alan said. "In the wild, if a mother whale can't hold onto the real newborn's body, she will find a net, plank, even a caribou carcass to carry as her lost surrogate calf."

As Mauyak swam slowly in circles, careful to keep the buoy-baby on the surface, as if to let it breathe, even the children watching understood this ritual of grief.

"That's her pretend baby," a young boy explained to his sister, without having to be told.

The small crowd was quiet, all eyes on Mauyak as she floated, making no contact with her mate, her female companion Shikku, her friend Alan, or the crowd.

"For almost a week after the delivery, she wouldn't look us in the eye," Alan murmured. "She's usually so gregarious."

I well remembered Mauyak's playful intimacies. In the spring of 1989, the first time I met Mauyak and the other whales, I'd been startled by their openness. They splurted me with water, opening vast mouths to take my hand against their tongues (their way of touching me), and allowed me to feed and stroke them. I was so happy to make contact with these whales closer to home, after a decade of swimming with dolphins far off in the Florida Keys. Also on that spring day I was fortunate enough to meet a tiny harbor porpoise named Magic who'd been found motherless, stranded on a Washington shore. This fine fellow, only the length of my arm, so trusted Alan that he allowed him to lift him in his arms briefly before splashing back into the pool. The next time I met Magic, a year later, he'd grown into a zoo favorite for his high-spirited antics. He was often let into the big pool with the three belugas, where he'd flirt shamelessly with them, sometimes being mistaken by the crowds for a little gray beluga baby.

The last time I'd seen Magic was in July 1992 when Mauyak was thirteen months pregnant, due in August. In stately maternity, Mauyak had kept her distance from the others, a lady in waiting. But Magic darted in between Shikku and Inuk. Stroking Shikku's white belly with his snout, snapping at Inuk over a float toy, Magic was all mischief. In a twirling ballet, he shot straight out of the water, dove deep, then nipped at Shikku's open mouth in a series of small kisses. From all this silly courtship, Mauyak held herself aloof, seeking solitude in the back pool. Did she anticipate then that she would deliver a calf destined to live only minutes?

"We know so damn little about belugas . . . especially their birthing," Alan said, stepping back from the pool to allow Mauyak her privacy. "Of the eight belugas born in captivity, only two have survived." He led us to the back pool for a closer look.

Even after twenty years of researching and working with dolphins and other whales, Alan believes we know only a quarter of what we should about cetaceans.

"The limits, you know, are not in the whales," he said. "They are in us."

He told of an experiment he had conducted with dolphins in which he placed eye cups on them and asked the dolphins to recognize certain symbols with their echolocation. "It took me months to design that experiment," Alan said, laughing. "And those dolphins learned the symbols in five minutes. So I had to devise a more difficult problem. But they just kept figuring it all out until I no longer had the technology to test their abilities. The last test I could design was discerning a symbol through sonar that was only one thousandth of an inch square. They aced that! While they were at it, they also identified different carbon densities in metal rods and differentiated colors."

Alan shook his head and led us into an enclosure with a giant plastic swimming pool. Inside raced a tiny dark porpoise, his dorsal fin no bigger than my three fingers. It was yet another stranded newborn porpoise, only several weeks old. The little one zoomed around the pool at the sight of Alan, his exhalations a tiny *twoosh* of moist air that delicately tickled my palms raised about a foot above the surface of the water.

Alan smiled wistfully and greeted the baby porpoise by making a series of sucking clicks and whistles. Delightedly the porpoise spun around, then dove and swam speed circles before surfacing for another stroke. The staff was hand-feeding him every two hours. They had not yet named him, out of superstition, in case he did not survive—as if not having a name might protect them from the pain of his loss.

"We lost Magic, you know," Alan said under his breath, as if to protect the small porpoise, with its cetacean super-ultrasonic hearing, from his words.

"I know," I said, remembering my first visit to Mauyak post-delivery, when I'd been shocked to hear that Magic had died only days after I'd last seen him flirting with Shikku, several weeks before Mauyak's delivery. That bright summer day the little harbor porpoise simply sank to the bottom of the pool, having succumbed to the cetacean's most dreaded death: drowning. Cetaceans will beach themselves rather than drown. The necropsy did not reveal any cause of death. Here was another mystery to add to the inscrutable beluga birthing process.

The Point Defiance zoo staff was still desolate after the loss of both Magic and Mauyak's calf in less than two months. It showed in the tender concern and tentative hope for this new porpoise's survival. As one of the women staff members said, "We're all grief-stricken. We did everything we could—the best technology in the country, the constant monitoring of everything from blood to water quality. But it was no good."

She paused and sighed, sadly. "It makes you wonder, doesn't it? It's too bad there isn't heaven for animals."

Her words disturbed me deeply. Why is it, I wondered, that our Western idea of heaven is a world in which everyone but us is extinct? Are we here below as above, unconsciously enacting a mythical heaven-on-Earth as we watch species after species die out? How did we get so separated from our animals that our religion imagines heaven to be a place where we live forever without animal companionship?

The older myths—Native American, pagan, and even Old Testament—are inexorably linked to animals. The Native American believes that animals and humans metamorphose between the worlds, shape-shifters and allies continuing a cycle as ancient and natural as salmon returning home. The pagans revered animals, such as the wise serpent; ancient Greeks listened to their Delphic Oracle python. The Old Testament God instructed Noah to build an ark to weather the end of the world by water. Back then God included all animals in this floating afterlife. But now we've dwindled down to our modern-day mainstream religion's concept of heaven for humans alone. How clearly does this mythology betray our isolation and loneliness here on Earth.

As I stood with the others at the Point Defiance poolside, watching the tiny surviving porpoise spin and twirl beneath our outstretched hands, I felt my sadness lift.

"He's so alive," I marveled. "He's *got* to make it."

"Some of the staff secretly call him 'The Kid,'" Alan said, smiling. "They believe if we name him, he'll stay with us. I mean, after all, it is quite a coincidence that this little calf was stranded only days before Mauyak's calf died. Some of us wanted to let this porpoise into the pool with Mauyak to adopt as her baby. But the vote went against it. We were just too afraid of losing another whale."

My hands were numb now from the cold water of the baby

harbor porpoise tank. As I gently slapped the water's surface, the calf lifted his glossy short black snout and shot between my palms. At that moment my friend laughed out loud and started taking pictures. I looked over at her standing by the beluga pool and saw her splashed from waist to feet.

"Mauyak did it," my friend said happily.

"Go for it," Alan said under his breath. "Mauyak's calling to you. Maybe she can play more with strangers right now than with the staff."

We left the harbor porpoise tank and leaned over the deep back pool where both Mauyak and Inuk were splurting water at our feet. Inside Inuk's wide-open mouth lay several fish, as if he were offering to share his supper with us. I was accustomed to Inuk's playfulness, but the astonishing change was in Mauyak. For the moment she seemed relieved of her mourning, just as she had left the red buoy-baby on the other side of the pool.

Here now she raised herself up by her pectoral fins and came halfway out of the water to lift up my hand with her huge forehead. The action reminded me of my cat when he wants affection. Happily I gave it, overjoyed to see Mauyak's openness. She slid gracefully under my outstretched hand in a leisurely slide. My open palm tingled with the cool, fast elegance of whale skin, like a scarf of wet, raw silk being pulled sensually through my fingers.

Whale skin is a marvel of sensitivity and skills—twenty times more sensitive than a human's. But cetacean sensitivity does not stop at the skin. Whales use echoes in their sonar to hear one another's bodies and therefore read each other's emotional and physical states. Humans have begun to catch up with cetaceans in the much more limited technology of ultrasound. But what we cannot duplicate is the extreme sophistication of whale echolocation. For example, echolocation is three-dimensional. Its vibrations can bounce off the inside cavities of the body, listening and gauging the echoes sounding from the brain, the heart, the kidneys, liver, and even ovaries. It is common among those who swim with dolphins to find them herding a pregnant woman away from the other swimmers, encircling her as dolphin midwives. Many women have first discovered they were pregnant while swimming with dolphins, before they or ultrasound could confirm it.

Recently, human technology has come up with Doppler echoes in our own sophisticated sonar. According to Alan Sutphen, a medical doctor who is also involved with cetaceans, from our own Doppler echoes we can hear "the flow of blood through the microscopic capillaries of the (human) finger . . . as a veritable roar." Sutphen goes on to say, in an essay in Joan McIntyre's collection, *Mind in the Waters*, that "cetaceans are aware of each other's health and general well-being. Cancers and tumors must be self-evident. Strokes and heart attacks are as obvious as moles on our skins." Along with scanning the physiological state, cetaceans have the ability to recognize emotional fluctuations such as "sexual arousal, fear, depression, and excitement."

In other words, there is no hiding place from such sophisticated scanning. What would it be like for humans if we lived in a world without clothes or skin to stop our sensing skills? We might all become psychics, able to see clearly one another's deepest emotions and inner body. The world of appearances would be replaced by an inner knowledge we can barely fathom, for it would be both sensory and emotional. In his novel *Easy Travel to Other Planets*, Ted Mooney describes a human-dolphin love affair by saying that "humans dream with their hands, only their hands, and so have cities rather than sagas, monuments rather than memories." In contrast, he concludes, the dolphin, caressed by a woman's hands, "recalled every dream their touch had caused his skin to dream."

Skin that echoes, skin that dreams—this is the whale skin I stroked in my first meeting with the great belugas. This is the astonishingly cool and elastic whale skin my hands have memorized. One of my nephews, whom I took swimming with the dolphins, once cried out, "She feels like cool honeydew melons!" That is the touch, but the elegant buoyance, the movement under the hand is harder to explain. When I stroked Mauyak's forehead, that huge oil-filled melon used for echolocation, its gleaming expanse throbbed and pulsed under my palm like a gigantic heart. I could watch that white dome expand and retreat like an undulant wave atop her head. Otherworldly is the only way I can describe this sensation—like meeting an alien mind that moves alongside mine, but so unfathomably. I can only rest my hand on such a mind as it works, scans and records and responds. All I know is that the feeling is utterly distinct, a blissful communion.

Perhaps it is true, as some researchers believe, that belugas and other cetaceans exist in an alpha state their entire lives. We do know that their brains never really sleep or slip into unconsciousness as do humans'. Because cetaceans must mindfully take each breath, if a whale loses consciousness it will drown. Only one hemisphere of a cetacean brain rests at a time. In the wild, scientists have observed pods of dolphins in which all those on one side swim with one eye closed; those swimming guard on the other side of the pod will have the opposite eye closed. So even as they rest one side of their brain, they are aware.

Continual consciousness, an environment that floats their bodies just as water floats our human brains, and a mind that never shuts down. What are they thinking all those hours in the ocean? How differently does their intelligence develop without using so much of their brains to operate hands as we do? Why do cetacean species rarely kill their own kind or, except for the orca when very hungry, devour their own kin? Do these big-brained mammals have something to teach us about survival, about altruism and consciousness?

These are the questions I mused over as Mauyak opened her

gigantic mouth to take my small hand, her pink tongue as soft as a baby's face against my palm. Her forehead throbbed, her great black eye opened wide as if to take me in, body and soul. My hand felt the rows of tiny round teeth tender against my skin. She held my hand, but she sounded all of me. And I trusted her with all my heart. With one flick of her mighty tail flukes this beluga could have bitten into my hand and bodily dragged me underwater, her massive thousand-pound bulk easily drowning me. But never has a beluga harmed a human. They treat us with the mothering kindness of a gentle giant toward a smaller species still struggling to understand.

As Mauyak held my hand in her mouth I wondered, Are whales somehow carrying our species in this world—the way whales will mournfully carry a calf or lift a newborn up to the surface for air? Are whales waiting with their cetacean consciousness for us to wake up from our long slumber—the dream in which we believe we are alone here, that we are the only minds at work on this planet? Do whales wait for us to discover the humility within ourselves to recognize our mammal kinship and then take the next baby step: apprentice ourselves to another species' way of being at one with the world? Can we learn to be co-creators with our extraordinary mammal kin?

Imagine a time when instead of zoos for entertainment and some slight education we had learning centers, where we'd enter a world without cages, without captive animals. We'd study animals through videos, holographic images, soundtracks, and books in preparation for field studies in which we would journey to the animals' wild homes, and in their habitat experience their different lives. After the initial animal research training we might sign up for safaris or swims with wild populations of cetaceans. Or we might join with Roger Payne of the Lincoln, Massachusetts, Whale Conservation Institute to study ocean toxins that threaten us all. Or sign up for a Bahamas trip with the Wild Dolphin Project out of Jupiter, Florida, to study and swim with elusive spotted dolphins. Or why not volunteer to help with the Caribbean "Into the Blue" dolphin-release project to restore captive dolphins back into the wild? Or journey to Brazil with Roxanne Kremer's Rosemead, California-based "Preservation of the Amazonian River Dolphin" project?

Already, organizations such as Earthwatch, in Watertown, Massachusetts, offer field trips to anyone interested in assisting scientists in the study of animals ranging from the Galapagos turtle to the South American jaguar. Apprenticing ourselves to animal intelligence would not threaten or disturb the current scientific study by trained experts. The programs would simply be state- and federally funded projects to facilitate the open classrooms that take students into the wild as an integral part of learning about nature.

How would this change our relationship to animals? Instead of the limited analytical point of view of a self-proclaimed superior species, we would experience what wild animal societies can teach us about communication, cooperation, and caretaking. We might also learn preservation of habitat—something about which our overpopulated, polluted, "civilized" society shows an astonishing ignorance.

Does our species really have the humility to learn from animals? We are at a crisis in our environmental relationships that begs for new models of thinking about ourselves and the world. We've been the "master race" for so long that our relationship with the planet and with its animals is like that of totalitarian dictators and their subjects. But with totalitarianism falling all over the world in the realm of politics, it's time for the Berlin Wall between our species and others to fall, too.

Centuries ago we believed that the entire universe revolved around our planet. Since then we've figured out that ours is one of many planets that revolve around the sun. It always takes our minds a while to catch up with scientific revelations.

Modern-day physics is telling us that if you look at something, you change it. How might simply looking at other species as equals change our future, our chances for survival?

The Bible predicts that "the meek shall inherit the Earth." I'd expand "the meek" to include cockroaches and pioneer rats and crocodiles—all veteran survivors, heirs to this blue planet. Is it possible for us to imagine a world that might one day select *against* our species in order to survive? The ancient concept of Gaia, the Earth Mother, has been revised in some scientific circles to declare that the Earth herself is a living, sentient organism ever balancing and maintaining herself. Another current theory is the "New Story," which tells the drama of this planet with Earth as the major character and humans as minor players. We may well strut and fret our little lives for not too many more generations.

Our fate as a species has always depended upon our ability to adapt and change in response to environmental exigencies. Only in the most recent centuries of reason and technology did we presume to separate our fate from that of nature and the other species. But Earth is changing, and it is our fate to adapt to this planet, not vice versa. Our religions must now remember this truth and celebrate again our dependence upon nature, our interdependence with all living creatures. If we can restore our perspective, we may well survive.

When we bring our hearts, minds, and myths into an open relationship with the natural world, we cease to be a dead weight that the world must carry. How long will nature carry us? Will the Earth, like those great whales, carry us until we disintegrate? Is the Earth, like that beluga mother, in mourning, grieving over the human part of herself that has died to her in our lonely lack of connection?

As my hand lay palm-open in Mauyak's huge mouth, I felt she held the whole of me—deeply, tenderly. Her eyes also held me: unblinking, utterly aware. I felt a great wave of grief wash over me, tears blurring my eyes. My heart opened and I felt the calm and clear stillness between us.

"I know . . ." I said softly. "I know."

Mauyak gently eased her mouth open and let my hand float in the water near her jaw. She turned on her side, without breaking our gaze. Then she slipped her huge head beneath my hand and I stroked her from melon to tail flukes. In slow elegy, the beluga swam across the pool to retrieve her floating buoy—the baby that will never disintegrate, the calf that could not stay in the world.

Let us stay in the world, I wanted to say to Mauyak. *Let my species and yours stay together,* kin here on this blue, sea-encircled planet.

Mauyak brought her buoy-baby back to me and drifted just out of arm's reach, again holding my eye with hers. We held that gaze for so long it seemed that together we held the whole world between us, as if our gaze was a gravity that kept the world spinning. And who knows what other worlds besides?

Looking at Mauyak, then as now, I believe that the beluga baby is as much alive in spirit as my own beloved grandfather, as alive as any of my species gone to another world. And when I join those of my human and animal family gone before me, I expect my afterlife to be surrounded by all species—from the serpents to the eagles, from the jaguars to the cockroaches. And in that afterlife of animals, that spirit-ark that carries us all alike, I'll look to swim alongside a gleaming bright beluga baby.

FISHING WITH FRIENDS

IN EARLY SEPTEMBER 1991 WHEN THE NORTHWESTERN light was late and lulling, I went salmon fishing for the first time. My friend Flor Fernandez offered to share with me the subtle fisher's art—part pole, part tackle, part meditation—that her father had taught her in the dazzling azure waters off her native Cuba. Using fish bait of humble herring, sardines, and squid, they coaxed from blood-warm Caribbean waters red snapper, yellowtail, and barracuda.

Fishing here on Puget Sound, surrounded by Pacific ring-of-fire volcanic mountains, was a far sea gull's cry from Cuba. But as Flor calmly remarked, "Fishing is flexibility. You flow, you drift, you troll, you go in circles, you rock, you yield to the currents. Fishing is a feeling, no matter what country you're in. In fact," she added, "fishers are people without a country. They belong to whatever body of water supports them."

After a decade of living on the shores of Puget Sound, I understand that I belong to this body of water. In the spring I set my ears to hear the bark of sea lions as an alarm clock; in the winter I watch for signs of a stray gray whale in midmigration. In the summer I take to the sound in a borrowed, battered wooden rowboat. But it had never occurred to me to fish there until that early autumn day when Flor arrived with her heavy-duty pole and a pound of frozen herring.

A net as big as another body lay between us in the boat. While Flor cut bait for a pole twice her height, I leaned back with a smaller one, oars lazily dipping in the water. Around us other fishing skiffs broke out bag suppers, while the motor-boats—one bedecked with a barbecue—cruised by with beer-can salutes. We floated in companionable reverie.

Suddenly, a pull from below. The pole was half out of my hands before I could begin to reel in the line. For several ex-hausting minutes I believed I'd snagged a sea monster; my arms were pliable as seaweed. Flor was no help. She had a big bite, too, and was wedging her feet against the boat to keep from being towed overboard. Then both lines went slack. We stared at each other, too breathless to speak.

"That," I finally got out, "was King Salmon."

Native Americans, I told Flor, say the first salmon is a visit-ing chief, and we must return him to the sea to make sure the Salmon People will keep coming back.

"But who can catch them?" Flor asked, stretching her sore muscles. "I'd starve to death if salmon were the only fish in these waters."

We did hook a rock cod and a sun perch. Though we got other mighty bites, it was obvious we weren't fishing for the wily salmon, we were feeding them. The sun tilted over the Olympics, and I rowed us home.

As I leaned wearily into the oars my ears pricked to under-water sounds, high-pitched squeals and clicks I half recognized before the water erupted into bubbles around our boat and we began to spin in a slow whirlpool.

"Orcas!" I shouted. "Everywhere!" I leaned over, plunging my hands into the roiling bubbles.

"We'll capsize!" Flor yelled.

I assured her that orcas don't attack humans, but Flor looked doubtful as our boat was sucked into the closing bubble net that herding orcas breathe to round up fish. Any minute a killer whale might have breached to feed, great toothed mouth gaping. I started singing at the top of my lungs (I'd heard that orcas, who have their own complicated language, respond to our music). As we swirled around in this eerie, churning eye, I heard a yelp. Flor had something on her line.

She effortlessly pulled in a shining coho salmon. At that moment the orcas kindly set us free. Black-and-white bodies slipped below, then surfaced far off with a *whoosh*, in search of other fishing grounds.

"It's the first salmon," Flor said. "The orcas caught it for us."

In the pale twilight she held up the elegant fish, its silvery scales glinting with their own light. Without a word she gently unhooked the salmon; it arched and dove back into the sound. We rowed toward shore, hopeful that the Salmon People would return.

DOES AN EAGLE PLUCK OUT
HER OWN EYES?—
BEYOND THE TRAGIC VISION

YEARS AGO, WHEN I FIRST READ JOSEPH MEEKER'S ESSAYS in *Wilderness* magazine, I was surprised to find that he belongs to the Northwest. But after reading an earlier book, *The Comedy of Survival*, and his essay collection *Minding the Earth*, I would think the Northwest proud to claim him. A writer of international and national repute, Meeker marries literature with ecology to search for "the healthy compatibility of nature, mind, and art."

The Comedy of Survival is a truly original study of how our Western inheritance of the Greek tragic tradition has led us to the brink of ecological catastrophe. Meeker states, "Tragic writers, like engineers, have consistently chosen to affirm those values which regard the world as mankind's exclusive property." This penchant for celebrating tragedy pits man against nature—both his own nature and Nature itself. In the Western tragic tradition, "personal greatness is achieved at the cost of great destruction." Tragic heroes are bent on transcending the natural order (and so life itself) to consciously choose their own moral order. We would not see, for example, a kingly eagle pluck out his own eyes as Oedipus does, to establish a moral universe. This inability to see nature past our own tragic projections prompts Meeker to suggest we put ourselves in truer perspective. "Spiritual and artistic creativity are not special powers provided so that humans can transcend the natural world," Meeker argues, "but features of human biological development useful for connecting humanity more deeply with the world."

Comedy or the picaresque tradition of not taking ourselves so seriously is what Meeker suggests might ensure our, as well as our Earth's, survival. From *Hamlet* to Dante's *Divine Comedy*, Meeker's book is a profound romp through heretofore unexplored wilderness where our stories and our ecology meet and dance and teach.

Continuing in this comic tradition, *Minding the Earth* is a series of trim, eloquent essays with titles such as "People and Other Misused Resources," "Irony Deficiency," "Nurturing Chaos," and "Living Like a Glacier." Calling on his trainings as scientist, professor of literature, ecologist, and writer, Meeker's essays are gems of unexpected synthesis.

Among conservationists these days, there is hot debate over exactly what our relationship to the Earth is. The seventeenth- and eighteenth-century man-against-nature attitude of early North and South American explorers or settlers, who stood vulnerable and all but lost in vast continents of primal forest, has given way to the less rapacious but perhaps equally antagonistic attitude of being keepers of the Earth. Federal agencies such as the Forest Service and the Bureau of Land Management have adopted this way of managing, or "multiple use" of the land. But this tradition is being challenged by such diverse movements as the radical environmentalism of Earth First!, the conservation lobbying tactics of groups like the Wilderness Society, and the more mystical, unifying vision of the Gaia hypothesis (in honor of the Earth Mother in Greek myth).

Meeker's slant is that of human ecology, the interrelated study of human and natural processes. The essays here speak to this current debate by embracing scientific, spiritual, literary, and philosophical elements. In particular, "Assisi and the Steward," originally published in *Wilderness*, invoked the wrath of conservative Catholics and fundamentalists and brought fervent praise from some other Christians. Through it all Meeker takes a calm, scholarly tone to deftly delineate the differences between the world's major religions and their ecological beliefs. "In three of the five major religions" (Christianity, Judaism, Islam), "images of human power and authority are dominant and the main theme is stewardship," writes Meeker. The original Old English word *stiweard* means "the warden of the sty . . . pig-keeper." In its current environmental coinage a "steward" is one who manages God's property on God's behalf. These religions believe that humankind will be judged on how well it oversees this worldly Garden. The Hindu and Buddhist religions also see conservation as a "spiritual necessity," though they teach interdependence among all living things, including the Earth itself. To these religions, spirit is as much in a river or tree as in a human body, and "usefulness to humanity is not among the criteria for evaluating nature." We are in a debate, Meeker concludes, over "whether nature belongs to us, or we to it."

Whether he is tenderly chiding us to laugh a little more at our grand notions of tragic dominance or praising the trillium flower that shows us "it is possible to be beautiful while still retaining the benefits of uselessness," Meeker reminds us of our cosmic choice to connect with, rather than tragically transcend, our Earth.

PRACTICING FOR
ANOTHER COMMUTE

I CAME TO LIVE IN SEATTLE IN 1981 DURING A NEW Year's blizzard; and I lived a month on Mercer Island without once seeing Mount Rainier. It was mid-February when I got my first glimpse of that mythical mountain—and it was almost the last thing I saw.

My friend Jo and I were driving across the sturdy, low-in-the-water bridge one midwinter morning. It was a glorious day, sun startling away those Seattle mists, which I knew hid a mountain that awed local folks like some fabled Isle of Avalon. But having myself lived high in the Rockies, I privately thought it somewhat amusing that so much was made in this city about hills and *one* mountain.

I was not prepared that morning to glance from oncoming bridge traffic to the lake and see a dazzling white whale breeching way up out of the waves—over the guardrail, breathing in the bridge, the whole horizon, all the air. I gasped and let go the steering wheel, turning to meet that mountain full face. It wasn't faith or terror that made my whole body turn toward Mount Rainier; it was more instinctive, like the way something vegetable in us faces the sun.

My car swerved, tires thump-thumping against the cement guard curb, then bouncing back to dart into the dangerous reversible lane.

"You never get used to it," Jo said calmly, reaching across and righting the steering wheel as simply as if we'd been playing bumper cars. "Not really. We just pretend it doesn't overwhelm us."

She was smiling, nodding to Mount Rainier as casually as if bidding howdy-do to a big, a really big, neighbor. But to me that day when I lost control of my car, my caution, my grownup and carefully contained capacity for awe, it was as if I'd seen the sky split open to reveal that god or goddess the child in me always believed lived in clouds.

For a year I commuted across the bridge; from my study at night I stared at the floating globes of white, the red zip of taillights, the bright, oncoming eyes of cars streaking across a dark expanse. Since the mountain was so rarely around, it was the bridge I memorized, in the way that we will commit to memory a certain road, or room, or smell that suggests a lover, a leave-taking, a life's change.

The Mercer Island Floating Bridge became for me that year a daily ritual, a kind of meditation, a movement between parts of myself. I dreamed about the bridge, made it my own, and so it became important in my life in a way I was not to understand fully until the end of that year and my time on Mercer Island.

That year my friend Jo died on Mercer Island. Death, like Mount Rainier, is a thing we never really get used to. As I was driving back across the bridge that day of Jo's death, the mountain was obscured by mists, but I saw and felt something just as amazing as Mount Rainier. I saw the faces of all those commuters—face after face after face coming toward me in waves.

And where before those faces had seemed wrapped in their

own mists, unknowable, now their humanity was no longer hidden. I caught my breath. How brave, how frail, how naked the faces seemed in that after-death aura Jo's passing left me. In those brief, passing faces I saw a beauty and vulnerability that broke my heart. Did they know they were mere mortal? Did all these commuters know that they might leave in the morning and never return—or return to find the fabric of their lives rent wide? How do we keep driving every day across this Mercer Island Bridge knowing how fragile the link is?

I started shaking, hands on the steering wheel, just like that day when I'd first seen Mount Rainier. I turned in its direction, looking for its massive, assuring solidness like a sign, something to steady me. Then I remembered Jo saying that we had to pretend the mountain didn't overwhelm us, as life does from time to time.

So I looked instead at all those faces, the brave and the sad and the wondrous and the weary who commute between life and death while a great mountain silently witnesses. And I finally felt what steadied my hands on the wheel: I felt the presence, though invisible, of that dispassionate mountain; I felt the stretch of the steel bridge like courage, like a human umbilical between what we know and what we believe.

Now when I commute across the Mercer Island Floating Bridge, I consider it practice for another commute. I keep my hands steady on the wheel, my car surely on the bridge—even when sometimes the sky splits open and, small as I am, I see something so much larger.

THE WATER WAY

IF LANDSCAPE IS CHARACTER, THEN NORTHWESTERNERS are most like water. We are shaped by the voluptuous shores and salt tides of Puget Sound, the deep currents of the Columbia, Salmon, and Snake rivers; finally, we are held back from falling off the proverbial edge of the world by a Pacific coastline whose nurturing rain forests and rocky peninsulas face the sea like guardians. Being surrounded by water, we cannot impose our own rhythms on nature as easily as a bulldozer does on a southern California canyon. It is we who find ourselves subtly in sync with the rise and fall of tides, the ebb and flow of the natural world.

This distinction—that northwesterners are more changed by their environment than it is by us—is crucial to understanding our character. Once, a convention of New Yorkers visited Seattle. On the harbor cruise to Blake Island, birthplace of Chief Sealth (Seattle), for a salmon feast hosted by Native Americans to re-create the first salmon bake and potlatch ceremonies that defined tribal life here for thousands of years, the tourists commented that everything seemed in slow motion.

"We've had to shift gears," said one New Yorker, somewhat anxiously. "Everything's so laid back. Maybe it's all those negative ions in the atmosphere."

Another visitor said, "How do you stand traffic jams on those floating bridges. Can't they just pave a part of Lake Washington?"

Finally, a rather pensive, bespectacled literary agent remarked, "Now I know why Seattle is singlehandedly keeping New York's book business alive. You have to go inside in all this gray and wet. I feel like I'm dreaming."

"Must be why Seattle has espresso carts on every corner and some of the world's best coffee." Someone laughed. "It's to keep yourselves awake!"

Northwesterners are a dreamy lot. We're in a fine tradition of dreamers. According to the Wasco Indians along the Columbia River, the tribe knew long before the white people came to settle at Alki Point, in 1851, that a change was coming. As told in Ella E. Clark's classic *Indian Legends of the Pacific Northwest*, one of the Wasco elders dreamed that "white people with hair on their faces will come from the rising sun." The strangers were prophesied to bring with them "iron birds that could fly" and "something—if you just point it at anything moving, that thing will fall down and die." They also brought new tools such as axes, hatchets, and stoves. Along with this new technology, the white people brought a philosophy of individual ownership of the land.

The Native Americans knew that the land could never be owned, just as it was impossible to section off the vast winding lengths of the emerald-clear body of Puget Sound, so like a watery dragon embracing the land. Even now, after over a century of non-Indian dominance, Puget Sound property rights ebb and flow according to the tides, not the set boundaries of so-called landowners. If even our ownership of northwest land is called into daily question by changing tides, how much more deeply are we affected by water?

Northwesterners not only reckon with water shaping our physical boundaries, we have learned to live most of the year as if underwater. Rain is a northwest native. Our famous rainfall is perhaps all that shelters us from the massive population and industrial exploitations of nearby California. The rain is so omnipresent, especially between late October and even into June, that most northwesterners disdain umbrellas, the true sign of any tourist.

Widely acclaimed Port Angeles poet Tess Gallagher tells it this way: "It is a faithful rain. You feel it has some allegiance to the trees and the people. . . . It brings an ongoing thoughtfulness to their faces, a meditativeness that causes them to fall silent for long periods, to stand at their windows looking out at nothing in particular. The people walk in the rain as within some spirit they wish not to offend with resistance."

One must be rather fluid to live underwater; one must learn to flow with a pulse greater than one's own. A tolerance for misting gray days means an acceptance that life itself is not black and white, but in between. If the horizons outside one's window are not sharply defined but ease into a sky intimately merged with sea and soft landscape, then perhaps shadows, both personal and collective, are not so terrifying. After all, most of the year northwesterners can't even see their own literal shadows cast on the ground. We live inside the rain shadow. We tolerate edges and differences in people and places perhaps because our landscape blends and blurs as it embraces.

There is a strong Asian influence here in the Pacific Northwest. Seattle's expansive harbor is a gateway to the Orient, and the strong, graceful pull of that more feminine culture is felt here. In fact, the classic *Tao Te Ching*, by the ancient Chinese master Lao-tzu, could well be a description of the Puget Sound landscape and character—we are flexible and fluid. There are not the rigid social strata of New England or the South. There are not the climatic extremes that make for a sizzling summer race riot in Watts or the violent cold of Chicago. Even the first Native Americans were known not so much as warriors but as fishermen. While there were territory battles, there was also a diversity and abundance of food that contrasted sharply with the southwest tribal struggles over scarce resources. Amidst this plentitude, northwest art flourished—so did storytelling.

In keeping with the landscape's watery changes, the northwest Native stories are full of legends in which animals change easily into people and back again. For example, the Salmon People are an underwater tribe who also spend a season on land; the whales and seals can metamorphose into humans as easily as the ever-present mist and clouds change shape. Many northwest coast tribes tell of merpeople, part human, part mammal, who mediate between the worlds to keep a watery balance. One of the most common gods was called "Changer." Many Native tribes began their mythologies with water— floods and seas creating what we now call "the people." A Skagit myth details this beginning, when Changer decided "to make all the rivers flow only one way" and that "there should be bends in the rivers, so that there would be eddies where the fish could stop and rest. Changer decided that beasts should be placed in the forests. Human beings would have to keep out of their way."

Here in the Northwest it is we humans, not water, who must keep out of the way. We pride ourselves on living within nature's laws, on listening to our environment before it is irreparably lost and silenced. It is, after all, here in the Northwest where the few last nurturing old-growth forests still stand, where people fight fiercely to preserve them for future generations. Here is also where the country's last salmon still spawn. But for all their strong conservation of nature, there are signs that even the "Rainy-Day People" are facing growing environmental challenges.

Oil spills blacken our beaches, and many species of salmon are endangered; gray whales are found on their migrating courses belly-up from pollution in Puget Sound. There have been major closures of shellfish beds throughout the region because of toxic contaminations from industrial waste. And, as always, the old-growth forest debate rages between loggers and those who struggle to conserve the trees.

The Puget Sound Alliance, a local program to protect Puget Sound, employs a full-time soundkeeper who patrols the shores checking reports of pollution. There is the highly acclaimed whale museum and its staff in Friday Harbor, who have been studying the transient and resident pods of orcas in the San Juans for many years. Greenpeace is highly visible in the Northwest, as are local grass-roots organizations formed to save well-loved forests and wetlands. There is a growing movement among corporations whose headquarters are in the West to give back some of their profits to protect our wilderness. Such bioregionalism runs strong in the Northwest. After all, many people moved here to be closer to the natural world. The urban sprawl of California, the East Coast penchant for putting nature in last place—this is the mind-set most northwesterners sought to escape and seek to guard against.

Just as northwesterners claim closeness with their natural world, so too are we close to our own history. Compared with the Native tribes, we are young. Our history here is only 150-odd years, compared with thousands of years of Skagit, Suquamish, Muckleshoot, Okanogan, and multitudinous other tribal roots. Some of these Indian myths calmly predict that "the human beings will not live on this Earth forever." This is an agreement between Raven, Mink, Coyote, and what the Skagits call "Old Creator." The prophecy predicts that human beings "will stay only for a short time. Then the body will go back to the Earth and the spirit back to the spirit world." The possibility of this simple ebb and flow of our human tribe seems more resonant here—here where the animals inter-change lives with the humans, where the mists can transform entire settlements and skyscrapers into low-hung cloud banks.

Our human conceits carry less weight in this watery world. Perhaps this is why during the first days of the Persian Gulf War, as during those seventy-two hours of the failed coup in the Soviet Union, it was remarked that there were more fishing boats on Puget Sound than usual. It is typically northwestern that this gone-fishing-while-the-world-falls-apart attitude pre-vails while in other areas of the country the population is transfixed by CNN. It is not that northwesterners aren't deeply involved, it's just that nature can be an antidote to such strong doses of terror. Nature can also remind us that there are other mysteries at work in the world, which might hold more power than our own. And more hope. Li Po, ancient Taoist sage, writes:

> Since water still flows, though we cut it with swords
> And sorrow returns, though we drown it with wine,
> Since the world can in no way answer to our craving,
> I will loosen my hair tomorrow and take to a fishingboat.

If water is our northwest character and rainy reverie our temperament, it follows that those of us who stay long in the Pacific Northwest must develop an inner life to sustain us through the flow of so many changing gray days. This means that ambition is not only an outward thrust toward manipulat-ing our environment; ambition may also be an inner journey, not to change but to understand the often unexplored territory within, what Rilke calls "the dark light." Are we a more mysti-cal region and people? Let's just say the climate is there and so is the water way.

KILLING OUR ELDERS

As a small child growing up on a Forest Service lookout station in the High Sierras, I believed the encircling tribe of trees were silent neighbors who protectively held the sky up over our rough cabins. For all their soaring, deep stillness, the ponderosa pines and giant Douglas firs often made noises in the night, a language of whispers and soft whistles that sang through the cabin's walls.

Several summers ago, a friend and I drove through those High Sierra and Cascade forests again on a road trip from Los Angeles to my home in Seattle. In the four-hour drive between the old mining town of Yreka in northern California and Eugene, Oregon, we counted fifty logging trucks, roughly one every four minutes. Many of the flatbeds were loaded with only one or two huge trees. On the mountainsides surrounding the highway, I was shocked to see so many clear-cuts, where once flourished ancient trees. Thousands of tree stumps bobbed across the barren hills like morning-after champagne corks.

I don't know when I started crying, whether at the sight of crazy-quilt scars of clear-cutting or when I saw the sullen bumper sticker in Drain, Oregon, heart of logging country, that read: WHEN YOU'RE OUT OF TOILET PAPER, USE A SPOTTED OWL! Maybe it was when we called our friend's cabin on Oregon's Snake River, outside of Merced, and he told us that every day, from dawn to dusk, a logging truck had lumbered by every five minutes. "It's like a funeral procession out of the forest," my friend Joe said. "It's panic logging; they're running shifts night and day before the winter or the Congress closes in on them."

As I drove through those once lush mountains, I noticed my fingers went angry-white from clenching the steering wheel every time a logging truck lumbered by me. I wondered about the loggers. They, too, grew up in the forest; their small hands also learned that bark is another kind of skin. Among these generations of logging families, there is a symbiotic love for the trees. Why then this desperate slashing of their own old-growth elders until less than 10 percent of these ancient trees still stand?

Amidst all the politics of timber and conservation, there is something sorely missing. Who are the trees to us? What is our connection to them on a deeper level than product? In the 500,000 years of human history throughout Old Europe, the pagans worshiped trees. The word *pagan* means simply "of the land or country." When we recognized that our fate was directly linked to the land, trees were holy. Cutting down a sacred oak, for example, meant the severest punishment: the offender was gutted at the navel, his intestines wrapped around the tree stump so tree and man died together.

Our pagan ancestors believed that trees were more important than people, because the old forests survived and contributed to the whole for much more than one human lifetime. Between 4,000 and 5,000 years ago in our own country once stood the giant sequoias in the Sierra Nevadas. Most of these great trees are gone; but in Sequoia National Park there is the General Sherman Tree. Thousands pay homage to it every year. And no wonder. According to Chris Maser in *Forest Primeval: The Natural History of an Ancient Forest*, the General Sherman Tree "was estimated to be 3,800 years old in 1968. It would have germinated in 1832 B.C. ... [it] would have been 632 years old when the Trojan War was fought in 1200 B.C. and 1,056 years old when the first Olympic Games were held in 776 B.C. It would have been 1,617 years old when the Great Wall of China was built in 215 B.C. and 1,832 years old when Jesus was born in Bethlehem."

How have we come to lose our awe and reverence for these old trees? Why have we put our short-term needs for two or three generations of jobs before our respect for our own past and our future? As we drove past the Pacific Northwest sawmills, I was startled to see stockpiled logs, enough for two or three years of processing. And still the logging trucks thundered up and down the mountain roads.

To quiet my own rising panic over such a timber rampage, I tried to understand: "What if trees were people," I asked myself. "Would we treat them differently?" My initial response was "Well, if old trees were old people, of course, we'd preserve them, for their wisdom, their stories, the history they hold for us." But with a shock I realized that the reason we can slash our old-growth forests is the same reason we deny our own human elders a place in our tribe. If an old tree, like our old people, is not perceived as *productive*, it might as well be dead.

Several years ago my grandfather died. An Ozarkian hardtimes farmer and ex-sheriff, Grandaddy was larger than life to the gaggle of grandchildren who gathered at his farm almost every summer vacation. Speaking in a dialect so deep it would need subtitles today, he'd rail against the "blaggarts" (blackguards) and "scoundrills" (scoundrels) he sought to jail for every crime from moonshining to murder. One of my earliest memories is playing checkers with a minor scoundrel in Grandaddy's jail. Another is of bouncing in the back of his pickup as he campaigned for reelection, honking his horn at every speakeasy and shouting out, "I'll shut ya down, I will, quicker 'n Christ comin' like a thief in the night!" I also remember Grandaddy sobbing his eyes out over his old hound's death. "It's just that he won't never be alongside me no more," Grandaddy explained to us. Somebody gave him a young hound pup, but Grandad was offended. "You can't replace all that knowin' of an old hound with this pup. That hound, he took care of me. Now, I gotta take care of this young'un."

My grandaddy's funeral was the first time I'd ever seen all my kinfolk cry together. Without reserve, some thirty-odd people in a small backwoods church sobbed—bodies bent double, their breathing ragged. It was a grief distinct from the despair I'd heard at the deaths of an infant or a contemporary. At my grandaddy's funeral, we all, no matter what age, cried like lost children. We were not so much sad as lonely. We were not so much bereft as abandoned. Who would tell us stories of our people? Who would offer us the wisdom of the longtime survivor? Our grandfather, this most beloved elder, was no longer alongside us.

When I returned home from the funeral, someone asked me, "How old was he?" When I replied eighty-six, this person visibly lightened. He actually made a small shrug of his shoulders. "Oh, well, then. . . ." He dismissed the death as if it were less a loss than if it had been of a person in his prime. I wondered if the man might next suggest that I get myself a new hound puppy.

The nowadays notion that people, like parts, are replaceable and that old parts are meant to be cast aside for newer models is a direct result of an industrial age that sees the body and the Earth as machines. In the preindustrial, pagan or agrarian society, the death of an elder was cause for great sorrow and ceremony. In our modern-day arrogance, we (numbers with value.

If, for example, my grandaddy were one of those old Douglas firs I saw in the forest funeral procession, would he really be equaled by a tiny sapling? Old trees, like old people, survive the ravages of middle-age competition for light or limelight; they give back to their generations more oxygen, more stories; they are tall and farsighted enough to see the future because they are so firmly rooted in the past. Old growth, whether tree or person, gives nurturing; the young saplings planted supposedly to replace them *need* nurturing.

As a nation are we still so young, do we still worship what is newborn or newly invented so much that we will be eternal adolescents, rebelling against the old order of trees or people? If our 200-year-old country were a 200-year-old Douglas fir, would we see ourselves as no more than prime timber to cut down and sell to Japan? Maturity teaches us limits and respect for those limits within and around us. This means limiting perhaps our needs, seeing the forest for the timber. If we keep sending all our old trees to the sawmills to die, if we keep shunting off our elders to nursing homes to die, if we keep denying death by believing we can replace it with what's new, we will not only have no past left us, we will have no future.

A Nez Percé Indian woman from Oregon recently told me that in her tradition there was a time when the ancient trees were living burial tombs for her people. Upon the death of a tribal elder, a great tree was scooped out enough to hold the folded, fetuslike body. Then the bark was laid back to grow over the small bones like a rough-hewn skin graft.

"The old trees held our old people for thousands of years," she said softly. "If you cut those ancient trees, you lose all your own ancestors, everyone who came before you. Such loneliness is unbearable."

Losing our old forests is like sacrificing many generations of our grandparents all at once; it's like suffering a collective memory loss. I could not help but ponder this vast loss when I read recently the sad reports of former President Reagan succumbing to Alzheimer's disease. In an interview, his biographer, Edmund Morris, reported that Mr. Reagan had stopped recognizing him—". . . I did not feel his presence beside me, only his absence." Morris then related a haunting scene: Referring to a set of his own Presidential papers, Mr. Reagan told Morris, ". . . move those trees." Morris commented, "Well, if a poet can compare stacked volumes to garners of grain, I guess a retired statesman can call his collected works trees if he wants."

Mr. Reagan was, of course, correct—his Presidential papers were originally made from trees. But the eerie coincidence is that he presided over a decade in which vast areas of our old-growth forests were cut down, and he is now, like those ancient forests, losing his memory. When I told this story to a South American who has spent many years studying with Brazilian shamans, she said softly, "Oh, your ex-president is like an old tree now, a grandfather who's fallen down and forgotten who he is." She shook her head sadly. "Old trees hold us to the Earth by their deep roots. And trees are our memories like the blueprints of our planet's history. When you cut those ancient trees, the Earth loses its memory, its way of knowing who it really is."

Our children's generation is growing up with only the memory of ancient forests; they don't feel the presence of old trees, only their absence. If we continue to cut down the ancient forests, will the Earth endure a kind of planetary Alzheimer's? Our forests, those brave and sheltering Standing People, need their ancestor forests, just as we humans need to be firmly rooted to our past generations, the grandparents who hold down our family tree.

I will always be lonely for my grandfather, the child in me

will always long for the Standing People who watched over me in my forest birthplace. On some spiritual and physical level our human entrails are still wrapped around the old trees, like an umbilical cord. And every time a great tree is cut, our kind die, too—lost and lonely and longing for what we may some-day recognize as ourselves.

Seagull Song

"Seagulls memorize your face," the old man called out to me as he strode past on his daily walk. I stood on the seawall feeding the flock of gray-and-white gulls who also make this Puget Sound beach their home. "They know their neighbors." He tipped his rather rakish tweed motoring cap and kept walking fast. "Can't let the heartbeat stop," he explained.

I meet this man many days on the beach. We rarely talk; we perform our simple chores; I feed the seagulls and say prayers, he keeps his legs and his heart moving. But between us there is an understanding that these tasks are as important as anything else in our lives; maybe they even keep us alive. Certainly our relationship with each other and with this windswept Northwest beach is more than a habit. It is a bond, an unspoken treaty we've made with the territory we call home.

For twelve years I have migrated from beach shack to cabin, moving along the shore like the Native tribes that once encircled all of Puget Sound. But unlike the first people who loved this wild, serpentine body of cold water, my encampments have changed with the whim of my landlords rather than with the seasons. Somehow mixed up in my half-breed blood is a belief that I may never own land even if one day I might be able to afford it. Ownership implies possession; as much as I revere this inland sea, she will never belong to me. Why not, then, belong to her?

Belong. As a child the word mesmerized me. Because my father's forestry work moved us every other year, the landscape itself seemed in motion. To *be long* in one place was to take deep root like other settled folk, or like the trees themselves. After I have lived a long life on this beach, I hope that someone might someday say, "She belonged here," as much as the purple starfish that cling to rock crevices covered in algae fur.

The Hopi Indians of Arizona believe that our daily rituals and prayers literally keep this world spinning on its axis. For me, feeding the seagulls is one of those everyday prayers. When I walk out of my front door and cross the street to the seawall, they caw welcome, their wings almost touching me as they sail low over my shoulders, then hover overhead, midair. Sometimes if it's been raining, their feathers flick water droplets onto my face like sprinklings of holy water. The brave fliers swoop over the sea and back to catch the bread in their beaks inches above my hand. Then the cacophonic choir— gulls crying and crows *kak-kak*-ing as my special sidearm pitch sends tortillas whizzing through the air, a few of them skipping across the waves like flour Frisbees.

I am not the only neighbor who feeds these gulls. For the past three years, two afternoons a week, a green taxi pulled alongside the beach. From inside, an ancient woman, her back bent like the taut arch of a crossbow, leaned out of the car window and called in a clear, tremulous soprano. The seagulls recognized the sun-wrinkled, almost blind face she raised to them. She smiled and said to the taxi driver, "They *know* I'm here."

It was always the same driver, the same ritual—a shopping

bag full of day-old bread donated by a local baker. "She told me she used to live by the sea," the driver explained to me once. "She don't remember much else about her life . . . not her children, not her husband." Carefully the driver tore each bread slice into four squares the way the woman requested. "Now she can't hardly see these birds. But she hears them and she smells the sea. Calls this taking her medicine."

Strong medicine, the healing salt and mineral sea this old woman took into her body and soul twice a week. She lived in the nursing home at the top of our hill, and every time I saw the familiar ambulance go by I prayed it was not for Our Lady of the Gulls.

Several years ago, when wild hurricanes shook the South and drought seized the Northwest, the old woman stopped coming to our beach. I waited for her all autumn, but the green taxi with its delighted passenger never came again. I took to adding two weekly afternoon feedings to my own morning schedule. These beach meetings are more mournful, in memory of the old woman who didn't remember her name, whose name I never knew, who remembered only the gulls.

Not long afterward my landlady called with the dreaded refrain: "House sold, must move on." I walked down to the beach and opened my arms to the gulls. With each bread slice I said a prayer that Puget Sound would keep me near her. One afternoon I got the sudden notion to drive down the sound. There I found a cozy cottage for rent, a little beach house that belongs to an old man who's lived on this promontory since the 1940s. A stroke had sent him to a nursing home, and the rent from the cottage would pay for his care.

Before I moved one stick of furniture into the house, I stood on the beach and fed the gulls in thanksgiving. They floated above my head; I felt surrounded by little angels. Then I realized that these were the very same gulls from two miles down the beach near my old home—there was that bit of fishline wrapped around a familiar webbed foot, that wounded wing, and the distinct markings of a young gray gull, one of my favorite high fliers.

Who knows whether the old man was right? The seagulls may have memorized my face and followed me—but I had also, quite without realizing it, memorized them. And I knew then that I was no newcomer here, not a nomad blown by changeable autumn winds. It is not to any house, but to this beach I have bonded. I belong alongside this rocky inlet with its salt tides, its pine-tiered, green islands, its gulls who remember us even when we've forgotten ourselves.

PERMISSION ACKNOWLEDGMENTS

"Gift of the Magi Cupcakes," "Stuff as Dreams Are Made On," "The All-Hours Lullaby Service," "Heartbreak Hotel," "The Evidence of Things Seen," "Practicing for Another Commute," and "Does an Eagle Pluck Out Her Own Eyes?" originally appeared in the *Seattle Weekly*.

"The Sacredness of Chores" originally appeared in the *Utne Reader* in a different form and in its entirety in *New Age Journal*.

"Beluga Baby" and "Sex as Compassion" originally appeared in *New Age Journal*.

"Fishing with Friends" and "Seagull Song" originally appeared in *Sierra* magazine.

"Killing Our Elders" and "Animal Allies" originally appeared in *Orion*.

"Vaster Than Empires and More Slow" originally appeared in the *New York Times* under the title "Hobos at Heart."

"The Water Way" originally appeared in *Insight*.

ABOUT THE AUTHOR

Brenda Peterson is the author of three novels and another collection of essays, *Living by Water*, chosen one of the best books of the year by the American Library Association. She lives on Puget Sound in Seattle.